TWISTED TALES

Thrilling Short Stories for Teens

AF517480

TWISTED TALES

Thrilling Short Stories for Teens

Dr. Manisha Kumari Deep

Bigfoot Publications

Because, there's a writer in everyone.

Twisted Tales : Short thrills for Teens
Author : Dr. Manisha Kumari Deep

First Published by
Bigfoot06 Publications (OPC) Pvt. Ltd.
B-10,12 Shree Shyam Palace,
Sector 4,5 Chowk, Old Railway Road,
Gurugram, Haryana (122001)
Website: www.bigfootpublications.in
Email: info@bigfootpublications.in

First Edition : August, 2023
© Dr. Manisha Kumari Deep

ISBN Print Book - **978-81-19512-10-2**

All rights reserved. No part of this book may be reproduced or transmitted in any form or by any means, electronic or mechanical, including photocopying, recording, or by an information storage and retrieval system—except by a reviewer who may quote brief passages in a review to be printed in a magazine, newspaper, or on the Web—without permission in writing from the copyright owner.

Although the author and publisher have made every effort to ensure the accuracy and completeness of information contained in this book, we assume no responsibility for errors, inaccuracies, omissions, or any inconsistencies herein. Any slights on people, places, or organizations are unintentional.

Printed in India

Disclaimer

This Short story collection "Twisted Tales: Thrilling Stories for Teens" is a work of fiction and imagination, written with an intention for readers to read and connect with the story. The content here has been presented just to make a fictional story for the readers to appreciate. None of the characters or plots have any resemblance to anyone living or dead. There are no beliefs or facts attached to it. The Author believes in all religions and faith and this novel is not written with an intention to hurt anyone. The Author respects each religion and faith equally. She makes no claim to the existence or authentication of any information presented in this story. It is purely a work of fiction and any resemblance to any person living or dead is just a coincidence. No claims related to any part of the story and any of its character will be entertained either by the Author or the Publishing house.

TABLE OF CONTENT

KATADESMOS

Repubblica di San Marino (Republic of San Marino), which survived the Renaissance and attacks in the 16th century, was now experiencing a decline in the 18th century, and attempts were being made to annex it to the Papal States. The Papal States or Church States were territories in Central Italy. The Popes had sovereignty over these states from 756 to 1870, and Julius II (1503-13), popularly called the warrior pope, helped the Papal States reach their maximum boundaries. However, in the early part of the 18th century, the papacy struggled to retain its powers. So in 1809, when the relationship between Pius VII and Napoleon became sour, the Papal States were once again taken under Napoleon's control. But Napoleon respected San Marino's sovereignty and liberty due to the intervention of one of his Regents, Antonio Onofri. He guaranteed to protect the independence of the Republic, which was instigated by the ongoing French Revolution and San Marino's refusal to extend its territories.

It was the first month of 1810, and San Marino was still enjoying its independence. However, poverty and its small territory were causing difficulties for the Sanmarinese people. Nonetheless, under all these odds, they were still happy because they believed that this was what was keeping them alive and preventing them from falling prey to larger territories. Although these handful of Sanmarinese were dependent on agriculture for their living, the

Vronti family secretly defended its borders from attacks and shared their agricultural produce with poor Sanmarinese families. They had settled in San Marino's territory during the initial reign of Pius VII and lived in the hilly part of Mount Titano. Surprisingly, they were able to grow enough produce for twenty families in San Marino.

Erinay and Neraida helped their father, Punraz Vronti, and Mother, Sara Vronti, in managing their small farmland and cattle. The people of San Marino loved the Vronti family for their generosity, even though they didn't know much about their past. The siblings played with the village kids and secretly learned warfare from a retired warrior. Sometimes, I also joined them. Erinay was very swift and strong, whereas Neraida was good at archery and communicating with animals. Other kids would laugh at Neraida when they saw her talking to her herd and birds because they couldn't understand their conversation and found it weird. Nevertheless, she could tell exactly when it would rain and when someone was entering their territory, making her the favourite in her family. Their mother used to shower all her love on Neraida. However, their father sometimes needed Erinay to plow their farm and take out the cattle for grazing. Erinay loved this time with his dad, and he was special to him. I envied it because I didn't get a chance to trouble him with questions, which he found annoying.

Gabriel the angel had told my parents that I was no ordinary girl and that I had a special purpose to fulfill in this land. But I could never figure out what it was until I met Erinay when I was five. The moment I saw him, I liked him. We used to play on the farms and ride on the back of bullocks. My parents were poor, and they used to sell items carved out of wood and dead animal bones. I was a quick learner and had learned this trade very well. But it couldn't hold me. I felt my calling somewhere else but didn't know where, so I spent time loitering around San Marino's town, meeting new people. Everyone loved me except Erinay. They used to say that my presence made their day, but Erinay never paid heed. I silently admired him, and maybe even loved him, but my small funny acts made him angry. But then again, that was who I was, and I couldn't stop being myself. I loved playing with birds and animals all day with Neraida, trying to learn her skills. She was twelve, and I was fourteen, but both of us made no sense to the fast-growing Erinay. He pretended to know everything and made silly mistakes egotistically, never admitting them. Neraida and I often had to come to his rescue. Yesterday, while he was swiftly climbing an oak tree, he broke a branch and slipped down from the top. We ran to the tree after hearing him scream and found him hanging from the tree on his leather belt, which we despised. Neraida called the great hawk to lift him and bring him down. But instead of thanking us for helping him, he frowned and said, "Now I know why I got stuck. You two were around this place and your spooky companion."

Dex the hawk whispered to Neraida, which she happily announced, "Dex says that if you are not happy, then he can put you back on the tree."

Erinay frowned and said, "As if I am going to spare your wings."

Dex swiftly picked up his sword and threw it away. He then flapped his wings, signaling Erinay that now it is payback time. He swiftly lifted him and placed him back on the oak tree. Erinay kept screaming and threatening Dex, but he stood beside us laughing while we girls were shocked at how things turned up.

"Tell him to say sorry, or else I will leave him hanging," said Dex mockingly.

"What will be the difference between you and him? Right now, you are stronger, but what if he shoots his arrow when you are flying?" said Neraida.

"Thanks for reminding me. But I am sure you will not let him do that," said Dex, looking at Erinay. Surprisingly, he picked up Erinay and flew into the air while we looked at them aghast.

"Boy's ride. Dex never gives me a ride."

"Michael, you always complain. It's not like that. You must be patient with birds and animals. Although I can talk to them, that was not enough to get close to them. When Dex was wounded by a hunter, I healed him back to health. That's what got us close. Then the news spread in the animal kingdom that Neraida is always there to help, unto this day. They are not afraid of me but love me," said Neraida, waving at them.

"I just want to see Erinay fly. It's his first real fight," I defended.

"Michael, do you like my brother? How do you remember every little detail about his life?" asked Neraida in amazement.

"I hope he could like me even as much as a chicken's feed. But can we just see him fly for now," I pleaded. Neraida made some hooting sound, and a giant owl came flapping down. I was awestruck as I had never seen something so beautiful.

Droid said, "Girls hop on. I will fly you safely."

I couldn't understand a word while Neraida said, "Gladly Droid. Thanks for coming, as always."

We both sat on Droid and soared up in the sky, listening to the delicate notes of the winds. It was my and Erinay's first flying experience. We were wide-eyed in amazement, trapped by the mesmerizing beauty from above the clouds. Time refused to halt, and it was almost late evening. Our stomachs were stuffed with wild berries, ringing with delight. Suddenly, I remembered that I had to prepare cornbread for dinner, and it was already late.

"Let's go. I must prepare dinner tonight."

Droid and Dex took a U-turn, heading straight for the farm to get rewarded with fresh corns. Surprisingly, none of the animals ate meat, nor did they fight with each other to keep Neraida happy. Animals occasionally died, and then the flesh eaters had a party, but Neraida refused to eat even dead meat. I never liked the flavor of meat and had never killed even an insect.

Juliet and Samantha joined us on the farm after Droid and Dex left.

"Where have you two been? Don't you have anything good to do? Why didn't you go to learn from Mr. Piero?" asked Aunt Sara, annoyed.

Erinay and Neraida sneaked into the home without saying a word.

"Go call your father, and you both better clean up before dinner. I don't want you all here for supper smelling like dead fish," she further added.

I walked home with Juliet and Samantha. On reaching home, I cleaned up and started kneading dough for cornbread. I had already ignited the wood-fired oven to bake cornbread, and the stew was boiling in the terracotta stove.

"Where were you all day?" asked my father, Francesco.

"Oh! She must be loitering around the town. That's what she is good at," frowned my mother, Mattian.

I was silent enough not to freak them out with my elaborate tale of my first flying experience with Droid.

"Is the dinner prepared?" asked my mother.

"Yes," I said and served supper to my family.

"I like the stew. What is this green grass that you have added to it?" asked Father.

"Where did you find this grass? Why have you kept this stone piece with something scribbled on it near the stove? Where did you find it? Doesn't it look old?" asked Mother, picking up the stone tablet.

"I found it in the forest."

I looked at that tablet with great pleasure as if I had discovered an ancient relic.

“Father, I found some fresh oregano leaves. I smelled them, and they were very fragrant. It was growing near this stone. So, I bought it for the stew.”

“I have never tasted anything like this stew. You cook even better than your mother,” said Father, slurping all the stew.

“Nice. She is learning fast. We must marry her in a year or two,” said Mother.

I raised my voice in defense, saying, “I want to learn more about the scriptures and stars. I don’t want to marry in a year or two.”

It takes two to tango, so father stood up and went to sleep in the backyard, saying that he was suddenly feeling very warm. I went to sleep with my mother. Lights were dimmed, and doors closed. The howling of wolves filled the dark night, and horrifying dreams of my marriage occupied my mind.

“Michael, wake up. Why are you sleeping till now?” said Juliet, shaking me up.

“What? It’s noon. I have never slept till noon,” said Mother, waking up hurriedly and running towards the backyard.

I ran to clean my hands and face to be with Juliet. She was waiting near the patio.

“Michael, have you seen your father? He is not there in his bed in the backyard,” said Mother, running towards the well.

“How was the door open? Didn’t you close it last night?”

“Let me ask Juliet. Your father left without finishing the work. We must deliver this piece of wooden jewelry to Mrs. Sara,” she said.

Instead of working on that jewelry, she rushed towards the patio, and I followed her.

“Juliet, have you seen Mr. Francesco?” asked my mother.

"I saw him talking to that strange lady who arrived in our town last night. She was picking up stuff from the market for free. They were so mesmerized by her beauty that nobody could utter a word. My mom and my brother Jack were angry at my father. He gave her one basket of berries that they had collected for our supper last night," replied Juliet.

"How can your father leave without informing me?" said my mother, weeping. "Oh! Mother, don't weep. I'll go find him. He must be in town for some work. Also, give me Aunt Sara's necklace. I'll deliver it on my way to the town."

My mother rushed inside to finish that necklace, and in a short while, we left with the necklace. On our way, we heard men praising that lady's beauty and women cursing her to be a witch. We finally arrived at Erinay's house and saw Aunt Sara giving fodder to the cattle. Erinay's dad was home for lunch from his farm, but Neraida was nowhere to be seen.

"Great noon, Aunt Sara. Here is your necklace."

"Where is Neraida? We haven't seen her," inquired Juliet, peeping around and behind the bushes as if she would jump out like a rabbit.

As usual, Erinay was busy sharpening his weapons and barely noticed me.

"Have any of you seen Mr. Francesco?" she further asked, and they all shook their heads in negation.

I was sad and hurriedly moved towards the town, inquiring about my father from everyone I met on the way, but nobody had seen him.

"Let's ask Neraida. Maybe she could help us," said Juliet.

We ran towards the forest as fast as our legs could take us.

On reaching the forest, I started shouting, "Neraida, Neraida."

“What happened? Why are you both so breathless? Is someone hanging on a tree again?” asked Neraida while making a perfect landing, riding on Dex’s back.

“Michael’s dad has been missing since morning. I had seen him talking to that strange lady who entered our town last night,” replied Juliet, looking amazed at the sight of Neraida riding a huge hawk.

Neraida whispered something in Dex’s ears, and he flew into the sky, soaring high out of our sight.

“Is she really riding that scary hawk? Am I dreaming?” stammered Juliet.

“Nope. You are not dreaming. She is riding the mighty hawk. It’s wonderful with Dex, Droid, Lilly, and all my friends in the forest,” I said, laughing lightly.

“I am scared to see it. I wonder how you both fly on it,” said Juliet, shivering slightly upon seeing Dex land.

“Come on. It’s not that scary. I am sure Dex will help us find Uncle Francesco,” said Neraida, and I breathed a sigh of relief.

While I was silently praying in my heart, a giant python started coming towards us in a wavy motion.

Juliet screamed on seeing the python and fainted. Neraida turned to look at what made Juliet faint. Suddenly, I had become braver and stood there looking at that beautiful yellow serpent with light brown patches. It opened its huge mouth to eat a wild fruit, and I started to tremble.

Even the python didn't disturb Neraida, and she said, "Nice to see you, Phygon. What brings you here?"

"I saw a woman today walking into the heart of this forest whose venom was worse than mine. She picked little birds from the trees just by looking at them and ate them alive," replied Phygon.

"I think she might be the same woman that Juliet was talking about. But how could she eat birds alive? I am going to throw her down from the sky," said Neraida angrily, and her eyes glowed with anger as if she would shoot fire from them.

Just then, Dex came and broke the news that my father was heading towards the church on the mountain near the cliff. I wondered why he was going to church at this time as we usually went on Sundays. Neraida whispered something to the oak tree, and it started shaking. Dewdrops from its leaves fell on Juliet, and she started to wake up.

"I should leave, else this girl will faint again. Anyways, I am coming with you. That woman seems to be dangerous. I can't let you go alone," said Phygon and slid away.

Juliet sat on the ground looking around for Dex, unaware of the presence of Phygon.

"It left. You run and inform the town about the woman and Mr. Francesco. They should come towards the church on the other mountain and must carry fire and weapons to defend themselves," said Neraida while lifting Juliet from the ground. She was still trembling with fear.

"Oh! My. Dex, you lift her in your claws and drop her outside the forest. Also, get my brother along with his weapons," said Neraida.

"No," screamed Juliet, but by then, Dex had grabbed her in his claws and was flying towards the town border.

Neraida started to hoot, and in a few minutes, Droid was there.

"I heard everything about Mr. Francesco. It is sad. But I am wondering that in a town full of young handsome men, why did that woman pick your dad?" asked the wise owl, which made me think hard about his question.

"He was fine. I cooked dinner, and we all ate together. After that, he said he was feeling warm and went to sleep outside in the backyard. He left in the morning without a word until Juliet came around noon and woke us up."

"What did you cook for dinner?" asked Droid.

"I made cornbread and potato stew using those oremint leaves that we found near that stone with ancient inscriptions on it."

"Let's go again and visit that place to see if something has changed," said Droid.

We reached that spot, but oremint was nowhere to be seen. Instead, that whole area was full of thorny weeds. There was no place for Droid to land, so he sat on a strong branch of a tree.

"How are you doing, Marvel?" asked Neraida, looking at the tree.

Surprisingly, this time I could hear the tree's voice but couldn't understand what Marvel was saying.

"When did these thorny weeds crop up? Were those here yesterday?" she further asked.

"The moment you all left this place with that herb and stone piece, these thorny weeds started to grow. It is stinky around and difficult for us. No birds are coming to sit on my branch and sing a song," replied Marvel sadly.

"I think it is due to the herb or the stone or maybe both," said Droid.

"I feel the same," said Neraida and explained to me the entire situation.

"Let's get that stone and leftover herb here."

"I think we should talk to my mother. She knows a lot about herbs and such stones. Maybe she could help us," said Neraida, touching my back lightly and caressing it to calm me down.

"You are right. No more wasting time. Dex might have dropped Erinay off at that spot. The villagers will be joining him soon. Let's meet your mom," said Droid, flapping his wings.

We both sat on Droid's back and flew to Neraida's home.

Aunt Sara was not amazed to see us land sitting on a huge owl's back.

"A few minutes ago, your brother left sitting on a giant hawk flying in the sky. I was at first surprised to see Erinay so comfortable riding a giant hawk, but I knew it was Neraida's magic," said Aunt Sara.

"What happened? Where did Erinay go?" she asked, looking at Neraida.

We narrated her the complete incident about father eating and then going to sleep. And how he went missing until Dex spotted him in the jungle going towards the church.

"Why was he going towards the church? Didn't Mr. Francesco inform his family before leaving with a strange woman?" whispered Mrs. Sara to herself as if trying to find some connection.

"We went to check the place from where I picked up some herbs and a stone with some inscriptions on it. The herbs have been replaced by thorny weeds. Marvel informed us that oremint changed to thorny weeds."

"Can you show me that piece of stone and oremint?" asked Mrs. Sara.

"I have it with me. Before visiting you, I went home to collect it. Here they are," I said and gave oremint and the stone to Mrs. Sara.

She stared at it in disbelief, flipping it back and forth and side to side.

"This is no ordinary piece of ancient stone. It is Katadesmos, a cursed tablet from ancient Greece. It is inscribed on it that Velma had been cursed for Lafi by Winci in the name of Hecate, the goddess of the moon and witchcraft. This Katadesmos had been buried with the grave of Velma's mother to make the curse more effective. According to these inscriptions, Velma cannot marry Winci's love Thutmose. Oremint is a magically poisonous plant used to inflict a curse on the chosen person," said Aunt Sara.

"Mother, now what? Will Michael's dad die? We are still unsure about curing the curse," said Neraida, looking at the Katadesmos.

"This is a limestone rock used to inflict curses for revenge or secret desire. So, if it was at Michael's home with oremint, which is called Pellagur, a magical plant used to initiate the curse, and it has been eaten by the family in the presence of Katadesmos, then the family is trapped in this curse. We don't know who that woman is or from where she has come. Michael, you go home and cook whatever you made last night using the same ingredients along with phar-hoo-roo herb, which is found near the lake in the forest. It is purple in colour with tiny blue flowers. Neraida, you will have to fetch this herb for Michael. I am going with others to the forest to bring Mr. Francesco home for supper. You both wait in Michael's home till we return, and I promise you that she will have supper with her father," said Mrs. Sara and picked up her axe while galloping on her horse towards the forest. She was a natural rider and a fighter.

I ran towards my home while Neraida flew on Droid to collect phar-hoo-roo from near the lake. My heart was pacing fast, and my legs were refusing to carry me. I fell and stood up again to run.

Somehow, I reached home and saw my mother sitting near the door weeping. I went near her and said, "Aunt Sara has told me everything. You wait here for Father, and I am going inside to cook. Believe in God, and everything will be alright."

With trembling hands, I lit the stove and wood fire oven. I reminded myself that I must cook the same recipe that I made last night with phar-hoo-roo magical herb instead of Pellagur. Half an hour later, I heard my mother screaming. I ran out to see Neraida and Droid. She handed me the curse reversal magical plant phar-hoo-roo, and I added it to the stew.

My mother fainted on seeing Neraida flying on Droid, and I sprinkled water on her.

She regained consciousness, and Neraida said, "It's okay, Aunt Martina. Droid won't hurt you. He is my friend. I am going to check on our people in the forest. I will let you know."

"I will come along. Please, I want to help you. This all is happening because of my foolishness. I must rectify my mistake."

"Hop on quickly," said Neraida, and Mom screamed, "This thing will eat you. I can't lose you."

"Droid won't eat me. Relax, Mom."

Droid flew high in the sky, and from afar, we could spot everyone, including my father. That woman was holding his hand. I felt anger raging inside on seeing another woman near my father.

"Let's go down and bash that woman. I can't stand it anymore. Whoever she is, I am not scared of her."

When we went near, the sight was unbelievable. None of the men were moving. They were staring at that woman and moving behind her, including Erinay. Women were crying and wailing at that sight. Droid hooted, and Dex screeched, but nothing worked.

That woman saw us and screamed, "Get me Katadesmos. I must take my Lafi with me."

"You can take your Lafi, but you will have to return my father and leave our town."

The woman started to growl, and her eyes started to shoot fire.

Seeing the trees burnt and animals scared, Neraida started to cry, and a few drops of her tears fell on the ground. Wherever her tears fell on the ground, fountains started to originate and extinguished the fire. With the sprinkles of water from those fountains, all the hypnotized men and quinceañero boys came to their true senses.

The Droid suddenly flew and grabbed my father in his claws and soared high.

Seeing this, the woman got angry and screeched, "Winci can't send petty girls to fight me this time. You can't defeat me this time, Winci. I will marry Lafi and take him home down the cliff."

My heart sank.

"Michael, she is Velma. How is she alive?" said Neraida, trembling for the first time.

"The same way your tears turned into a fountain to blow out the fire and wake up the hypnotized."

I turned and saw Velma running in the air.

"Am I daydreaming? How can she do that?" said Neraida.

"I don't know. But I am equally scared. Hold on tight," said Droid and suddenly started to catch pace with the wind, still holding my father tightly.

We were racing for my home to prepare supper to reverse the curse.

The Droid stopped outside our gate. We dragged my father inside, who was not willing to come. I was wondering when he would be himself again. My mother came out crying and hugged my father. Velma threw a fireball at my mother. Aunt Sara heroically jumped in to save her.

"She won't stop. Michael, take your parents inside and serve them supper," shouted Aunt Sara.

"Mother, come with us. You might get hurt," said Neraida, crying.

I couldn't believe how many families had been put in danger because of my stupidity.

"Neraida, you are a strong girl. You must save this town. Take Mr. Francesco inside and serve them supper quickly. Sprinkle some water on him to wake him or forcefully feed him," said Aunt Sara.

We dragged my father with my mother's help. Neraida rushed in to get some water to sprinkle. She came with a pitcher full of water. I looked at her, doubting her intention of sprinkling water.

She looked at me questionably about what I was thinking. I took a handful of water and sprinkled it on my father, but nothing happened, which made us wonder if he really needed to be soaked in cold water. From outside, we could hear shouting and screams. We had to figure a way out quickly, or else the next scream could be ours. I suddenly picked up the Katadesmos and placed it in my mother's hand. She started to cry and leaned to kiss her husband. Surprisingly, he woke up after my mother's kiss, but Velma had reached inside. Her eyes were glowing with anger, and so were mine. Nobody could separate me from my father. I wasn't scared of that dead woman anymore. Aunt Sara threw her deadly axe at the witch, but it passed through her body and got stuck on the wall. She was already dead. How will an axe kill her? Erinay had been wounded fighting her viciousness. Fearless village women started to arrive with fire in their hands and surrounded Velma. She angrily looked at Mr. Vronti when he growled at her, shaking her. I instantly fed my father and mother one spoon of the stew containing phar-hoo-roo, praying for it to cure the curse. But before I could swallow, she held me by my neck, and I screamed in pain. Neraida ran to help me but tumbled over a pitcher of water, which fell on the limestone tablet Katadesmos, and so did Velma. I fell to the ground and saw a smoky image of Velma screeching out of fear. Without a second thought, I ran and broke the Katadesmos. At twelve o'clock, I could see that smoky figure turn into a pretty woman who stood there with folded hands and teary eyes. But it was futile for me as she had dared to kill my family and friends.

"Thank you for freeing me from this curse, Michael. I was stuck in this limestone tablet for thousands of years. You freed my soul. Now it's time for Winci to return to hell for tormenting me and inflicting me with this curse," said Velma, and she faded into thin air.

Everyone looked at me disbelievingly, finding it difficult to accept that a clumsy girl saved them all. But the credit was not mine alone to take.

I hugged my friends and family and thanked everyone for standing there for us during this difficult time. We prayed together and thanked God. Women and men went home as couples with their kids, and I got my family back.

I went inside to get some turmeric to apply on Aunt Sara and Erinay's wounds, which miraculously started to heal.

On seeing her wounds heal, Aunt Sara said, "Michael, your hands are magical on wounds. Look how it's healing. I thought that I lost my leg and wouldn't be able to ride again."

"I am grateful to you all for helping me save my family. I am not sure about the magic part, but I'm happy that I could be of some help."

Aunt Sara hugged me and collected the broken pieces of Katadesmos. She went near the burning terracotta stove and threw all the broken pieces, chanting in some ancient language, "Frip Innanlands Senn."

The fire blazed high, burning every piece of the tablet. Instead of fumes, we saw red clouds leaving the room and fading up in the sky.

"It means 'sleep in peace,' and now neither Velma nor Winci can trouble anyone again. I just pray that Velma could meet her Lafi in another world," she said, and they all left.

"Sorry," said my father, and we cried before going to sleep.

Waking up in the morning seemed like a dream after the Lafi attack episode. I saw my parents kissing each other passionately, and somewhere I thanked those cursed witches for reminding them of their love. I went out to see the beautiful sun smiling at me and felt the morning sweet breeze.

"Time for daily chores," I reminded myself and went to get wood with my brother. The forest seemed surreally calm and unpleasant. I ran my eyes from one end to the other in search of Droid, Dex, or Phygon, but none were visible. We were walking inside the forest, picking dried wood and twigs when suddenly Jack screamed. I ran to be with my 10-year-old little brother and saw him running in the opposite direction. I ran faster to catch him.

"Where do you think you are going?"

"Mummy," he mumbled.

"Show me."

He clutched me tight and walked me near that place. I was horrified seeing a white, sucked-up, bloodless body and suddenly 'Crash.' I was lying flat on my face with something heavy falling on me. I crawled out using a tree bark and freaked out seeing that there were more such dead bodies. I closed my mouth tight with both hands and screamed. There were more bodies in trees. This is why the forest smelled like a graveyard. Without flinching, I ran behind Jack and saw Droid coming down to help.

"Droid, you have to lift Jack."

The next instant, I heard Jack screaming, and I was smiling. We landed on the Vronti family's farm, and Aunt Sara said, "Right in the morning, you are flying. No plans for work. What's wrong with Jack?"

Neraida and Erinay joined our conversation, and I said, "Did any of you visit the forest today?"

They nodded in negation, and I continued, "You all have to come with me."

Neraida hooted, and Dex swooped to soar high. In a lickety-split, we reached the spot, and every person had a cold foot.

"When did this happen?" asked Mr. Vronti, and Droid said, "last midnight."

"Last midnight, father," repeated Neraida for us.

"Who did?" he further asked.

"An old woman who was screaming Velma. There were many shadows in the dark that were following her," chirped Droid.

Neraida repeated it for us, and while we were dumbfounded, Droid's tiercel made a magnificent landing near him.

"Good morning, Macy. It's always delightful to meet you. Are the babies hatching anytime soon?" said Neraida, touching her beautiful red tail and gorgeous wings.

I noticed that she was bigger than Droid.

"Between all the commotions last night, the little ones hatched. God knows better about their timing. I requested Phygon to guard as I am in a dither," said Macy, despising the smell and dead bodies.

"Don't tell me you saw people flying?" said Neraida, and we alternately looked at them, trying to figure out the conversation.

"Worse," she said and continued.

"What? You saw these dead bodies dropping from the sky and then ghostly shadows leaving them to follow a walking dead woman. I can't believe it. How is it possible?" said Neraida, and we froze.

"This is much graver than we anticipated," said Aunt Sara.

"She was shouting, 'Where is my daughter Velma?' and picking up animals to drink their blood," said Macy.

"She is Velma's mother, Venice. How come she didn't leave this land after Velma?" said Aunt Sara, aghast.

"How did the stone come here from Egypt?" asked Uncle Punraz, and his wife replied, "Travelers. Someone intentionally dropped Katadesmos here. The evil spirits will kill innocent lives, and the nemeses will emerge victorious."

"You burnt the broken pieces of Katadesmos. How will we kill these walking dead?" said Erinay, who had been inspecting dead bodies for some clues.

I saw Aunt Sara missing and, in a blink, she was standing there again.

"How did you do that? Are you all magicians? How did you get that stone?" I said, stammering.

She looked into our eyes and said, "Velma and Winci are back. Francesco is in danger, and we have hundreds of them."

"Why did you do this?" I cried, and so did Jack.

"Kids, we will make it this time also," she said, holding us.

"How?"

"Collect all the scattered dead bodies and place them on a wooded pile. We will burn them, which will bring the evil spirits here," said Mr. Vronti, trying to count.

"Are you planning a feast for them?" asked Erinay, irritated.

"Do we have an alternative?" he shouted.

"Who will fight? Our wounds have not healed. Are you planning to fight them alone?" questioned Erinay.

I took the Katadesmos from Aunt Sara and touched their wounds, feeding them phar-hoo-roo from last night that I had in my pocket. The wounds magically healed completely.

"How did you do, Michael?" asked Aunt Sara in amazement.

"I had this queasiness that if this can hurt, then maybe the reverse is also possible."

Aunt Sara started to read the Katadesmos again and found the location of Venice's grave.

"Neraida, you will have to fly to Egypt and get Venice's grave here to burn with these mummies," she said.

"Why do you think that burning will kill these walking dead?" asked Erinay.

"This is because limestone cannot melt, but it can be burnt at high heat. We will burn this Katadesmos with it," replied her mom.

"You are assigning this job to our kid. Do you think Neraida is ready for it?" said her husband.

"Time and challenges will prepare them. You are forgetting the basic code," she said, and I stood there, wondering how we will fly to Egypt and return with the grave in twelve hours.

"Is there some spell on that stone to bring that grave magically here?"

Aunt Sara flipped it around and saw a note saying, 'This curse will remain until Thutmose doesn't marry Winci.'

"I guess my father is Thutmose, and he is supposed to marry this dead woman. We must hurry else we won't be able to save him."

We heard footsteps behind. Some villagers were there, and they were holding fire and water.

"What happened? Did you all know about these dead bodies?" asked Aunt Sara.

"Velma is back, and she has taken Francesco to the church to marry him," said Victor, panting for breath.

"We are late," said Aunt Sara.

"What if Winci marries Thutmose, and the curse is complete?" she said oddly.

"What if something else happens?"

In the middle of this chaos, I saw Neraida sitting and meditating.

"What are you doing? What is that huge bird in the sky?" I asked, petrified.

The ferocious bird landed in the middle of the forest, and Jack closed his eyes while running around.

"Thank you, Daniel, for coming to our rescue," said Neraida and touched that ferocious bird.

"I know your concern. Sara's guess is right. Francesco was Thutmose, and nature has revoked the curse long forgotten. There is only one way to undo the curse," said Daniel, and I was still lost in the thought of a bird talking, and we could all understand.

"What is it?" asked Neraida, impatiently.

"I will light the fire, and you add his blood to it along with the limestone. It is quite possible that he will remember his past," said Daniel.

"How do you know all this?"

"Daniel is the great dragon. He is thousands of years old and has seen many dynasties fall and rise," said Neraida. My misconception about birds being harmless and adorable went for a walk on the ice.

"I need men to collect these dead bodies and skeletons to put them on a huge pile of wood. We will burn them and send them to hell," said Uncle Punraz, and all the men got down to work.

I left with Aunt Sara, Jack, and Neraida to save my father. Daniel was majestic to ride. Even in this distressing moment, I was looking at that beautiful white scaly skin and long tail. But when it was about his ginormous saw-toothed face, all the beauty that I could see vanished.

"When will we reach? I am feeling scared."

"Stop behaving like Jack and pick your weapon to fight. Daniel will not eat you," said Neraida, and she showed her friend the church. Daniel smoothly landed outside the church, and we ran inside to save my father.

"Is she not afraid of Jesus? How can she enter the holy place?"

"They are evil souls but believers, and" before Aunt Sara could finish her sentence, she started to choke. We stopped to look behind and saw a ghostly woman with fangs holding her by the throat.

"Get your father here. He is mine. Velma can't marry him," she shouted.

"Who are you?" shouted Mr. Vronti.

"Winci," she replied.

"Only Velma is there with my father, and she is not evil but ironically still a soul. What will happen if she marries my father?"

"I know what you are thinking," said Erinay and threw his cross on her. Winci screamed and started to burn in a red flame. Mr. Vronti picked up the humongous cross placed at the church door and ran towards the army of the dead. Seeing their bravery, others gathered courage to walk with their crosses and chase them to their destiny. Aunt Sara, Neraida, and Jack entered the church with me. Velma was holding my father's hand, and the priest was reading verses from the bible. Aunt Sara ran with a small knife and cut the skin of my father's fingers. Blood dripped on the limestone, and it started to glow. We started hearing screeching, and the church was filled with the dead army, including Winci and Velma's mother, who were making their way back to the Katadesmos. Aunt Sara was holding it tightly with all her might while screaming in pain to not let go of the Katadesmos. We were holding each other, trying to avoid the wrath of ending up inside the Katadesmos. The church was empty, and I could see my father standing in front of my eyes but still holding Velma's hands, who was now a real woman.

"How can this be possible?"

It was like an evening spent in these dead people's reincarnation and leaving us at their mercy.

"You revoked the secret prayer that I had made while sacrificing myself for my love, Thutmose. If the curse fails, then I would come to life, and Thutmose will be mine," she said, kissing my father, and surprisingly, he said, "Yes, my love."

"What about my mother?"

"Only I can be with your father. So sadly, she had taken my place in this curse," she said, and my father smiled.

"What's wrong with you, father? You don't care for your wife and kids. Is this woman so important to you that you sacrificed your wife and our mother for her?"

"I remember you children and Mattian, but I can't do anything. Sara stopped this curse, and things went wild," said my father.

"I forgot to mention the tiny little detail that you were a witch but a good one in your league. Where is your goodness now?

Your desire to be Thutmose's wife has sacrificed an innocent life," said Daniel.

"You are still alive," said Velma, stroking Daniel.

"I want my mother," shouted Jack and ran out of the church.

Unexpectedly, my father followed him, leaving Velma.

"I am there for you kids, and I am really sorry about how things went wrong," said Aunt Sara, and Daniel added, "You are not alone to be blamed. Maybe this was destined, and I couldn't see it coming."

"How could you forget this detail?" I asked.

"He wanted his son back. You know fatherly love. His son James had been sacrificed by Winci to enact the curse," said Velma, and I cried, "Daniel, you are a monster."

"Father," said James.

Daniel hugged him and said, "Let's go home, son," and they were soon lost from our sight.

I sat there weeping for my mother, who had to face the wrath of my doing, and my father left with Velma, unaware of his kid's feelings.

"Don't cry. I have a way, but you will have to be strong," said Aunt Sara.

"I will do anything."

"Then go with your father and be good to Velma," she said.

"You will have to promise me that you will return."

"I can't let you do that. Your magic has not been tested through time," said Uncle Punraz, holding his wife close.

"You guys have magic," I said amazed by this revelation.

"Shush! You will alert Velma," said Aunt Sara, and I understood my part. I stood up and started running behind my father and Velma, holding Jack's hand.

"Don't leave us, Father. I promise we will not be in trouble," I said sobbing.

"They are your kids, my dearest. I don't mind having them along," said Velma in a freakishly cordial tone, which made me confident that next was my number to be sacrificed.

"Thank you, my love," said my father, and I refused to believe what magic could do.

"Thank you, Velma, for being so kind to us," I murmured.

We all walked together towards the village, while I slyly turned to look behind for Aunt Sara and Uncle Punraz, but could only see Uncle, Erinay, and Neraida. Tears rolled down my eyes, and I silently prayed for her safety.

It was night, and then morning until five days had passed, and still, there was no sign of Aunt Sara. I started to blame myself for all these happenings.

"I know what you are thinking. Every day, I think that I could fly on Droid's back and help my mother. I didn't know that Daniel would betray me," said Neraida while picking an acorn.

"I feel sorry that I can't help you, Neraida," said Marvel, and Neraida hugged her.

It was getting late, and so we decided to head home when a sudden gush of wind touched us precipitously. We turned around to see what trouble had landed again but couldn't hide our happiness on seeing Aunt Sara. Neraida ran to embrace her mother, and I stood there watching the family reunion.

"Mom, how did you find it?" asked Neraida, looking at Katadesmos.

"Arrange for your father and Velma's wedding in the church. She is a powerful witch, so be careful. By now, she might have felt that her curse has been tampered with," said Aunt Sara.

Droid came for our rescue, and we flew high after collecting flowers from the birds and inviting the animal kingdom to do decorations in the church. Meanwhile, I went to call the father of the church for my father's wedding, with tears in my eyes. Everything went as planned, and I saw my father and Velma near the church with our people. Aunt Sara had already come there and hid a dagger under her belt.

"Why are you hiding a dagger?"

"This is the same dagger that Velma used to reverse Winci's curse, and now we will kill her after the wedding to bring your mother back," replied Aunt Sara, and I gazed at her in disbelief. I knew my mom would be back.

2 STRINGS ATTACHED

23rd December 1990, Argentina

The transition of weather from spring to summer was best in the foothills of the Andes, where nature changed its form faster than a peregrine falcon, making it rethink boasting about its speed. This year's Christmas was special because I was meeting my cousins Leonardo, Hugo, and Jamaica after ten long years due to the sudden disappearance of my mother before Christmas. My father blamed his brother Albert for keeping the Tipler cylinder in functional mode that night. My dad's secret laboratory stopped functioning since then, other than him trying to trace my mother somewhere in this solar system at a different time. People laughed at his imagination and the possibility of my mother Britney's return, which was beyond the understanding of many. In my blurry memory, I clearly remembered the enthusiasm on my dad's face when he came to fetch wine and steak for himself and his wife that night. He wanted her to see his success, though she couldn't ride on it and time travel to a different century, as this was his Japanese-funded project for a private company in Japan. My father Joseph had an interest in physics since his childhood, and so did I. This is why, instead of supporting his father Finch and Spanish mother Mattia in agriculture, he became a physicist. His absence was filled by my mother whose knowledge of plants, animals, and food was commendable.

It was 23rd December 1980, around 8 pm when my mother went down to my father and uncle's secret laboratory. My father, with Uncle Albert, had successfully assembled together all the parts of their baby 'Tangerine,' which was heavy beyond imagination, and they were hopeful that using thunderlight, they would fire up the cylinder, landing it somewhere in the 1800s in the past. While they were rejoicing in their success, Mother stepped inside their humble aboard to inform them about Christmas dinner with the extended family the next day. She was surprised to see them happy after years. My Uncle quickly left to give my parents some quiet time with each other, while my father was boasting about his project. He then left to get refreshments for them while my mother was looking around in amazement. She found Tangerine's door partially open and stepped inside, which suddenly closed, and before my father could do something, she was out of sight. Father screamed for Uncle Albert, and together they tried to trace Tangerine in the 18th century, but she was nowhere to be found. They sat there weeping, and my father blamed my uncle for hastily leaving the time machine functional. The next morning, the news came that a woman was sucked up in a spectrum of blue and red light seen by a few for a fraction of a second. Every year since 24th December 1980, I flip through the same news of my missing mother in the newspaper kept carefully in my dad's side drawer. I knew that she wouldn't come back from wherever she was, alive or maybe dead. After this weird incident, my uncle had relocated to another end of the country to escape from the memory of this disastrous moment and face my dad's agony. But this year, Christmas was not gloomy like a Grinch; instead, Santa was planning to come down the chimney. I was having a blast with my cousins, unaware of our meeting with the truth.

Our day started with running down the hills and ended with stargazing on a clear night, trying to spot Venus or some constellations from our telescope. It was something new for Leonardo, who was more interested in designing new stuff like a camera that could capture images in space, and for Hugo too, who had an interest in the human body and medicines. Our fathers didn't consider us ordinary teenagers chasing pretty girls and horses. I and Leonardo were fifteen, while Hugo was a year older than us. Jamaica was already dating at seventeen, and her boyfriend was visiting us for Christmas. This was something odd and unusual for us, who didn't have time to give some attention to Jessica and Alabama visiting our farm and demanding to spend some time with us. Grandmother and Aunt Julian spent their days in the kitchen and farm, while we explored our interests and shared hobbies. This time Grandmother wanted us to help her with decorations and cookies. The flavor of Christmas cookies soaked in Dulce de leche sauce was a nourishment for a strained mind and thirsty soul. Our age-old family cookie recipe was being executed by none other than Jamaica under my grandmother's supervision. Aunt never made these cookies for Christmas as Uncle Albert would refuse to eat them without his complete family on Christmas. I saw a smile on my father's aging face after ten years when he met his brother and his family. I guess his wounds had started to heal as he was spending some time with Stephanie, a widower. Stephanie owned a shop in the farmer's market. I didn't like her much as the thought of having a stepmother and an older stepbrother disturbed me. I assured myself that this was just an infatuation that would fade with time.

Late evening arrived, and grandmother announced that this Christmas, I would have to celebrate my birthday, forgiving myself as it was not my fault, but a bizarre incident in which my mother went missing. After my father's yearlong effort to trace the prototype of Tangerine, which vanished with my mother, I decided to revisit the past. With trembling feet and wobbly hands, I started walking towards our basement lab, which had been closed for eight years. My father had given up his desire for exploring time travel after his wife went missing and he couldn't find her. From then until now, he kept himself busy on the farm, and his parents couldn't have been happier with his decision. Memories kept repeating in flashbacks, with tears rolling down my face; I couldn't hear footsteps approaching me.

"Where do you think you are going?" asked Hugo, shaking me hard from my jogging in memory lane. I looked blank, and Jamaica said, "Come to meet my boyfriend Bieber. He has arrived and wants to meet you all."

"Your cartoonist can wait. Please be with him and keep him busy while we find out where Antonio is going with a broom," said Leonardo, holding my hand.

"I'm coming along with you guys," said Jamaica, and we glanced at her in disbelief.

"I'm going to the lab. I want to decorate it for this Christmas and will celebrate my birthday there where my mother stepped for the last time. I can feel her there," I said, wiping away my tears. Jamaica ran to the balcony to get three more brooms with her, and this time she was accompanied by her boyfriend. We didn't know how to react, so we managed to give a faded smile.

"Don't waste time, as we will get late for dinner, and Mother will get angry waiting for us to join the family table," announced Jamaica, and we nodded in unison.

"Don't be shocked, and do not reveal this little secret of ours to anyone."

"Are we going on some treasure hunt?" asked Bieber, surprised, and Hugo responded, "Better than that."

The giant door creaked open with loud mechanical thumping, and the clock went tick-tack, reminding me of the same time ten years ago. The place still smelled like my mother's flowers in her hair. I stared around like a five-year-old child searching every nook and corner as if my mother might just jump out from nowhere, like Jamaica's cat Kitty. Lights went zooming, and cobwebs hanging from the ceilings and dusty corners were evident. "Get down to work, guys."

None of us noticed Kitty entering behind us. Bieber restarted Dad's computer and his semi-functional systems. The screen beeped with coordinates on the screen, and we moved closer to read it. "What is it?"

"I think these are the coordinates of the last search," replied Bieber, and I was speechless as it dated back to the day my mom disappeared. "How do you know?"

"My dad is a physicist, and he keeps talking about these stuff and Hawking's principles. I visited observatories and space research centers with him and learned about these machines. But there are more advanced versions. How come you guys have legacy systems?" he replied, prompting me to boost my dad and uncle's abilities in the field. I stepped forward and opened a gigantic mechanical door behind which was Tangerine. I didn't expect her to be there. I was just going to boast about her, showing that empty space.

I stared at her, and Hugo said, "Your mom was inside the prototype."

I stood there speechless, as if I had already made a full-proof blueprint plan.

"Don't freak me out," said Leonardo, as if he already read my mind, and I said, "You caught me, bro. Let's do it. Fire up the baby."

"I don't think it's that easy. Do you know how much power this thing would need? How will..." and before Bieber could finish his sentence, Jamaica had clicked on the location.

The next minute, we were lying unconscious toward the gate.

After a few minutes, I regained consciousness and started to wake the others up.

"What just happened?" asked Hugo, and Jamaica said, "Tangerine is still there. We failed."

We looked sadly at each other and dusted ourselves, but promised to come back to clean the mess the next morning. It was dinnertime, and before entering the dining room, we swore to keep this a secret.

"Kitty didn't eat," said Aunt showing us her bowl.

"This has never happened. I will go check on her," said Jamaica, and we stood up to leave.

"I'll help you," said Bieber.

We kept feeding ourselves like hungry wolves who had to chase deer with fear. After half an hour, Jamaica and Bieber came there empty-handed. We looked at them puzzled, and they said in chorus, "Kitty is missing. I think some wild animal ate her. She used to run into the woods often. I am sure this time she couldn't return," cried Jamaica.

Leonardo poked me and whispered, "I think we will have to go to the lab again. I left my camera somewhere."

"Seriously now. Everyone will get suspicious, and Jamaica is already crying. Bieber came today, and we already did plenty for him. Enough troubles for a day."

We went to console Jamaica, but Kitty was her childhood pet, and she wasn't ready to stop wailing. Finally, we gave up and went to our rooms.

Next Morning

"Wake up sleepy head," pinched Hugo, making me scream with his creepy voice.

"I want my camera," said Leonardo, and I said, "You want it at five in the morning. It's not going to fly anywhere."

But it was no use resisting as they dragged me to the lab. I was surprised to see Bieber already working his fingers on the keyboards and tracking device.

"What are you trying to do? Will you fry us this time?"

"No. Come and see this," he said, shocked, and we rushed towards him.

"These are the second coordinates but the same," he added, and I couldn't believe my eyes, "Tangerine did work, but what got teleported?"

"Kitty," shrieked Jamaica from behind.

There was dead silence. We had accidentally teleported an animal to the 18th century, and now she couldn't come back like my mother. One thing was for sure that my mother did get teleported, but what was baffling me was how come Tangerine was left behind, and her prototype vanished.

"I guess you are thinking what I am thinking. A bunch of teenagers teleported a cat to the 18th century. The experiment was a success, but reverse travel is not possible."

"I want my Kitty back or send me there. Who will feed her? What if some animal eats her?" shouted Jamaica, and we stared at her unbelievably.

"Are you serious?" asked Bieber, and she nodded.

"First help us in cleaning this place, and then fill our bellies, because with an empty stomach, my mind doesn't work."

We got down to work with super speed. While others were rejoicing in success, I was fighting with ethics, whether to reveal this secret to Dad or not because his experiment did work, but at the wrong time. My dad will kill me if he finds out, but what if he is happy with Stephanie and doesn't want my mother back? My heart skipped a beat as I had found an answer to escape an unescapable situation.

"Guys, who all are dying of hunger?"

Everyone raised their hands, and we went for breakfast. Grandmother and aunt were busy decorating the feast table, and we had to eat outdoors under the beautiful sun. My thoughts didn't leave my mind, making my favourite pancakes with maple syrup tasteless, forcing me to think if I was suffering from ageusia. Jamaica was mad at us for her cat, and I couldn't imagine a carefree girl like her travelling to the 18th century for her cat. I was forcing my limits to be her, and suddenly jumped on my two feet, announcing that I was travelling with Jamaica.

"We thought Jamaica was joking about travelling in time, but you are behaving like her. Don't you know what happened to your mother and Kitty? Aren't you thinking about your dad? Hasn't he lost enough?" said Leonardo angrily, making my brown cat eyes blurry with tears.

"I know, but still, I want to try to bring my mother home."

"They are physicists and then also they partially failed. We, a bunch of teenagers with superficial knowledge, want to run a failed experiment. We will end up in the mental asylum instead of the 18th century, unsure of which country. I hope there is no cerebral impairment due to unconsciousness last night," said Hugo, almost choking over food in nervousness.

"I know what I am doing."

"Then we won't let you do it," said Bieber with folded hands and continued, "I can't tell you how exultant I am feeling to know you guys. I can relate to your feelings, Antonio, but what you both want to attempt is suicide."

The abstinence of sound reminded me of a vacuum in space, and somewhere my heart was urging to pay a visit to my mother.

"Instead of presumptions about anything, first let us try to trace Leonardo's camera as it has a tracking device."

"Do you think 18th-century people used electronic chips for tracking? How do you think we will be able to track signals?" asked Bieber, and there, back to the void.

"I am going to stare at those coordinates again. If someone wants to…," and I clogged my eyes reading the headlines, "Last night again the same pattern of lightning was spotted as seen on 23rd December 1980 in which a woman disappeared."

"Are you reading what I am reading?"

"Don't you think if reattempted tonight, it might invite unnecessary attention?" said Leonardo, and I couldn't have agreed more, as maybe Dad read this news.

"Run…," I shouted in panic.

By the time we reached, Uncle Albert was going through the data on the computer screen.

"This time Kitty went. I hope she meets Britney," he said with teary eyes.

"I want to go to find Kitty," said Jamaica.

"None of you are going," said her dad.

"I want to find my mother, and you can't stop me this time. Tell me how this thing works."

"We were still working on it for time travel, waiting to capture lightning. We also don't know what happened that night. Why haven't we seen those lightnings again without firing Tangerine?" said Uncle.

"Uncle, it's Tipler and not Tippler. I am sure you and Dad will find answers and bring us back."

"Bring us back? What do you mean by this?" asked Uncle, and the systems started to beep with red alert.

"We have an intruder," said Uncle, and he saw signals coming from the same coordinates.

"Can we try to bring back Mom?"

"Your dad will kill me. I can't...," and before Uncle could finish his statement, Dad completed him, "You are right. So, you take care of him in case I don't return."

I instantly felt like a mouse doubting my dad's feelings for my mom.

"No. I will go. It was my mistake, and I want to correct it," said Uncle.

"Nobody is going anywhere. I am going."

"We will come with you," said my cousins, and I was wordless.

"I can't lose both of my sons nor allow one to go," said Uncle.

"This time capture that high-intensity light. I feel there's more to Cherenkov's light, maybe an undiscovered spectrum. It might help us land back Tangerine," said Dad.

"You don't have a choice, Antonio," said Uncle, but I defended, "Do you realize if this light beam is detected so soon again, we might come in notice, and this project of yours and mom's disappearance will be revealed to the world."

"Your disappearance won't be revealed. Is this what you think?" asked my dad, and I didn't have an answer.

"Let's design a high-intensity light detector to understand the nature of this light, which flashes to wink. Then we will start Tangerine and teleport you to the past," said Uncle.

"I haven't done anything which is against the law. This was a classified project, and there is no harm if it is revealed to the world. But I am going to the 18th century," said my dad.

"Great, but after the feast. Please don't make relatives suspicious," said Uncle, and we agreed. Dad and Uncle stayed back to work on the signal while we left to help Grandmother and Aunt with the arrangement.

"Grandmother, can we talk?"

"Why not, Antonio?" she replied.

"I want to go with Dad."

"Where?"

"Time travelling to mom."

"Have you two gone rogue?"

"Dad wants to go alone to find Mom. I too want to go with him."

"Nobody is going anywhere. I have tolerated enough of this. Losing Britney wasn't enough that now I must lose you both," she said and started to sob.

"Dad won't listen as he knows that Kitty got teleported to the same place that he had planned to run a dummy trial where unfortunately Mom went."

That very minute Grandmother rushed towards the lab, and we ran behind her. But when we reached there, the scene was different.

"Where is Joseph?" she shouted.

"He wasn't ready to listen, so I teleported him to the same coordinates where Britney and Kitty went," said my uncle sobbing.

Grandmother came and started to hit her son on his back.

"Mother, I will do something to bring them back. Give me some time," he said crying.

"What will you do? You both couldn't do it together then, and now you are saying you will do something," she said and sat on the floor crying.

"It's daytime, and the unusual light in the sky would be less evident. This is why we chose this time. We are ready to reveal Britney's absence to the world," he said trying to comfort his mother.

"I want to go there too. What will I do alone?"

"You are the offspring of my son. I can't risk you," said my grandmother, but her words and tears couldn't dissuade my determination.

"I promise you that I will return safely home. But now my parents need me."

"Okay, tomorrow after you celebrate your 15th birthday with us," she said, finally giving in to my demand.

The feast was quite a hush-hush event, and everyone noticed the absence of my father. Grandmother was as silent as death, and nobody questioned her about the whereabouts of my father. I was eating with my cousins and Bieber on the lawn to avoid eyeballs. That evening's sundown didn't have the hope of a shining tomorrow. I knew somewhere that maybe I wouldn't return home, but the desire to have a home away from home was more tempting at this moment. I had decided to travel to the 18th century with the first dawn the next morning.

25th December 1990

The cake-cutting ceremony was oddly mute, with occasional cutlery clanking and munching to fill a hollow belly. I was eating more than usual with the fear of dying due to hunger reaching my parents. At last, the moment arrived for me to pay gratitude to my mother for feeding me cow's milk and loving me unconditionally, which made her absence grow with each passing day.

"If we don't return, then assume that we are in someplace better. Please do not cry your whole life over it," I managed to babble sobbing.

"Wait. You said that they will come back. I can't lose my grandson," said my grandmother, whose grief could be clearly seen in this dense foggy morning. I stepped forward and hugged her to leave. Tangerine looked at me as if derationing my abilities and mocking at my decision, making my feelings of death stronger. Like a stubborn-headed, hasty, nasty teenager, I stepped inside her, trying to prove her wrong, as if it would justify my sensibility and sensitivity. Uncle started the engine, and I waited for my doom. Before we could realize it, Leonardo ran to me, and Tangerine closed her door for the outer world.

"Are you mad? Why did you come to lose your life, leaving your family behind to cry?"

"I came for my cousin brother, who is no less than my siblings," he replied, and we held each other tight in this last moment. Tangerine's ongoing spin on her longitudinal axis was already making us dizzy, and we were wondering how we would survive her billion spins per second. I was sure that Mom, Dad, and Kitty must have vaporized, and so would we. Our cheeks were flying, and I felt that we were spacewalking at a gargantuan speed in a circulating beam of light. We looked at each other shockingly, trying to realize the thinning line between life and death. Were we dead, and was this our soul being taken to heaven for trying to find my parents as a reward for our selfless love? Somewhere we were content that at least we would land in a good place with angels if not heaven. The imagination of that good place and life there began to fill my mind with thoughts of living with parents again along with my dearest cousin. Time was spinning in my head, and I decided to open my eyes when my guardian angel arrives to guide me to my home.

After Some Time

Antonio wakes up. "I think we are in hell," he said shrugging me from unconsciousness.

"What are you saying? I thought we are not sinners as we never dated and broke a girl's heart or left a baby unattended or brutally killed an animal or chased out a hungry person or…," and I stammered, "This ugly place looks worse than our polluted Earth. Is there something called a bad place between heaven and a good place?"

"What are you saying, Antonio? I know you got a hard blow on your head, but this idea of yours is absurd. Let's walk ahead and see what is there," said Leonardo, pulling me up. I felt my stomach churning, and I vomited half-digested cake and pudding. We were feeling thirsty and exhausted.

"Are we still alive, or after-death people feel thirsty and exhausted?"

Leonardo stared at me and said, "I am no God to answer your questions. Let's find it from someone."

We finally gathered our leftover soul that was tight and intact, retaining its shape after this strenuous journey and found ourselves standing near a forest. Before we could figure out what to do next, a pair of hands grabbed us from behind and made us smell some flowers. When we woke up, we were inside a cave. I slowly mourned with pain as if torture in hell had begun.

"I knew you would come," said a familiar voice, and I looked up and saw a woman who somewhat reminded me of my mom.

"Are we in a good place or a bad place? Have you met angels here? How is the food? Where is my family?"

"Your father told me that you will follow him here. It has been ten long years since I left you behind and prayed each day to meet you again," said that woman.

"You have been very brave, Antonio," said another familiar voice, entering the cave, and I turned my head to figure out who he was.

"Dad, you are alive. I am so happy to find you again."

"And I am happy to find your mom alive and safe. I told her that you are rock-headed and will surely attempt to follow me. I didn't expect you, Leonardo. Your family might be worried for your safety," said my dad.

"You both are also my family. I couldn't have let Antonio go through this alone," he said, and my father hugged his nephew for his courage and generosity.

"I am indebted to you, my son," he said, kissing Leonardo on his forehead like a kid.

"Where are we? Is it the 18th century like you anticipated?"

"No, son. We are in the 25th century," he replied sadly.

"Oh, Dad. This is incredible. I thought we were dead, and this is our afterlife. But we are in the future. You and Uncle did a fantabulous job."

"You are right, son, but what is intriguing is that we travelled through the light, which was no ordinary beam of light but cosmic radiation from an unknown Cherenkov spectrum. I am still wondering how to return to Earth."

"Dad, now we have to time travel to the past as we are on Earth in a different phase of time."

"What if we land at some other time? How long can we hover in this thing?"

"You are right, Dad, but let's not give up hope."

"Are we in Argentina?" asked Leonardo.

"No. We are in China, which is under alien rule. All the Chinese and foreign nationals on this land and two-thirds of the world have been taken over by them. I think our time travel has some connection with them," said Mom.

"How are you so sure about it?" asked Dad.

"I have been hiding in these forests like stone age people. Hunting for food and taming wild animals and predators to protect me from these two-foot aliens," she replied.

"Tell us more, Mom."

"These tiny super brains have flying saucers to monitor, and their transparent nets carry thousands of people in a jiffy, filling their prisons and making them work in the most inhumane conditions one can imagine. They have laboratory-grown and breed species of dinosaurs and mammoths. I heard that they used the gene sequence, bone, and cells from fossil remains to develop them again. They are a little altered, as different forms of lizards and elephants were used for this experiment. These animals are allowed to free roam in their habitat, and any human who dares to escape is thrown into these animals' laser cages. I had once seen it with my bare eyes. They have the least security in these forests as they have nothing to do with oxygen," said Mom.

"What do you mean by 'Nothing to do with oxygen'?" asked my dad curiously.

"Unlike humans, they do not breathe oxygen but resemble plants except that they always breathe carbon dioxide. This is why the more the pollution, the merrier for them," replied Mom, serving us some water from a pitcher.

"When did you see them first?"

"I landed inside this cave and fainted outside it. After I gained consciousness, I found myself surrounded by wolves. Suddenly, a man jumped in the middle from nowhere and saved me. I asked him where I was, and he told me that we were in China. He taught me a few survival tricks and helped me hide Tangerine in this cave. There are some gorilla warriors who are fighting these Trudence. Their hair is dense like the top of trees with leaves and branches. They have eyes, a nose, a mouth, two hands with ten fingers each, two legs with broad feet, and three toe fingers. They solely depend on robots and technology for survival against humans. Some people have been heard saying that they have a mother tree hidden in their base to which all of them are attached. They have the fiercest warriors guarding them in robotic suits. If someone can reach there and kill that tree, peace will be restored on Earth," replied Mom.

"I wonder why China," said my dad thoughtfully.

"Like we humans have colonized other planets in our solar system and exploited them, these Trudence are no different. Chinese people's advancement in technology and greed for more made them targets of these aliens. The country which proudly declared to colonize Mars is now a slave and has also dragged the whole world into this mess," replied my mom.

"How will we reach there?"

"If it's 'Tree of Life,' it needs light. You can try this light detector that I and dad made to detect Cherenkov's undetected spectrum. I hope this might help us," said Leonardo.

"Do you have a clear lake or pond? I will make a larger version of this and place it on top and one near the lake to capture the beam of light," said my dad, examining that detector carefully.

"I am sure that Lorenzo might provide us with an advanced version of the same," said my mom.

"That will be risky. I will use a primitive style that will not intervene and can go undetected," said my dad.

"You are right. So, use the silicon inside your giant baby to trap light. It is 31st December 2499, and you want to use primitive-style technology," said a voice from behind.

"Hello, Lorenzo. It's nice to see you," said Mom, and I saw an unusual happiness on her face.

"This is a graviton stimulator and detector which will simulate cosmic light and detect its path," said Lorenzo, giving Dad a large device that looked like a multimeter with just a computer monitor attached to it.

"How do you start this?"

"We will use it at night when there is no sunlight and Trudence's real-life source can be detected. This is a very old device as now nobody can own technology and must use technology terminals for the same on pay-per-use basic. It seems that we are in the 19th century," he said, and we were aghast at his comment.

"Trudence have travelled through time by joining two parallel cosmic strings, and this is how they reached here," he further added.

"What about us? How did we land here?"

"This we can know by discovering their base station," he replied.

"This is no ordinary cave but a type of meteorite which contains silicon and gravitonium metal. This is why the Tangerine prototype landed here. Why didn't I notice it earlier? Moving in space-time fabric is much simpler now. Wait for the nightfall, and we will surely find the light source of Trudence. I will gather my men and attack it," he said, carefully looking at the cave walls.

"We will teleport to that light source and not just detect it," said my dad, which made us speechless.

"Alone it might be risky," suggested Lorenzo, but Dad was determined.

We rested for a while after a healthy meal and waited for the night. With the howling of a wolf, I woke up and shook others from their sleep. Leonardo started a graviton simulator and connected it to Tangerine's prototype.

"We have limited time in which we will have to reach their base and destroy it. Else this time, she will teleport alone," said Lorenzo, touching our prototype.

"We are ready," said Mother, picking up her deadly axe and passing one each to everyone.

We closed our eyes, and before I felt I would puke again, we fell on a red sandy surface. We looked around but couldn't spot a soul.

"Where are we?" and mother started to poke me, pointing in the opposite direction.

We saw the most gigantic time grid of space-time travel with every switch connecting to a delicate space-time fabric. It was unbelievable.

"What the hell is this?"

"This is how Trudence came to China in the 25th century," replied Lorenzo, and I continued his statement, "And even if they finish us in the 25th century, they can travel forward or backward in time anywhere and never die, though their planet is dead. This second hand which moves once a year decides their stay on a planet in that time frame. The only thing alive on this planet is that golden tree."

Everyone glanced around to spot that tree and found it near the 31st-century switch. The switch pattern was like the electricity switches that we have in our homes through ginormous. We were searching for the source of that ginormous rotating time clock.

"How do we stop this thing? It is very clear that they have travelled from the 31st century of the time on this planet to Earth. This planet was destroyed, and with this space-time travel technology, they are alive since thousands of years, travelling backward or forward in time," said Leonardo, pointing at the marked clock timing pointing at different centuries on different planets.

"This means they cannot revisit that place again. They always must choose a different century to invade, and then they devastate it. This is their nature. They are parasites and always search for a new host to survive. They pollute the environment," said my mom.

"This is why it has started to rain carbon in China and around the world. Slowly life will finish due to excess carbon, and then they flee in their spaceship to a new timeframe. So smart of them," said Lorenzo.

"If they die, this golden tree will die. But how do we kill them?" said Leonardo, and suddenly Kitty came running and sprang on him.

"Jamaica will be thrilled to have you back, Kitty," I said, picking her up.

"True, but only if we kill this thing else, we are about to die," said Lorenzo, and Mom interrupted him, saying, "Not so soon. Let's teleport them to the ice age in Antarctica. No food and extreme cold. They won't be able to survive, and when parts of the tree start to wrinkle and die, automatically this tree will experience slow death."

Her answer was like lightning out of a summer sky. Instantly Dad and Lorenzo started to climb that clock tower.

"Be careful," shouted Mother.

"They will take a lot of time to travel there," and before I could finish, Lorenzo threw a rope, tripping down the short arm handle from the 25th century and triggering it to Cryogenian age around 850-635 million years ago. He then came down laughing. We pulled Dad down and ran to the same spot where we landed just in the nick of time to be teleported back to our cave. We heard sounds of freedom and rejoicing. We ran outside our cave and saw Trudence spaceships leaving Earth. Nobody knew our little secret.

Lorenzo hugged us and said, "Thanks for helping me in saving my planet," and Dad patted his back, saying, "Our planet, my friend."

"It's time to go home, Mom."

Dad entered our home coordinates while Lorenzo changed the source to join two strings to power our system and said, "We also have little secrets not exposed to the world. This is why Trudence chose us. Sometimes technological advancements can be a curse."

"Do visit us, Lorenzo," I shouted, and he waved, smiling.

Everyone was lying here and there, sleepy with swollen eyes because of crying. Kitty sprang on Jamaica. I saw the Christmas tree and said, "I am sorry, grandmother, for being a day late for Christmas dinner."

CRAZY LITTLE DREAM

Living in the countryside of San Francisco had never been this gloomy, where shadows left my side to borrow more time for me from the jaws of the dark. My invisible faith had tried hard to join the broken ends of my family, not anticipating that the devil was mocking me. All my enthusiasm had drowned, and I was trying to glow with some borrowed light. Not because my funny three-eared and five-legged friend didn't help me fix loose ends, but because this evening betrayed me. My only friend in this long stretch of green hills and the farm was missing. Even when my parents fought, I never cried; losing my bedroom to eight-year-old Fiona didn't bring down my spirits; carrying my deliberately broken bicycle for repair couldn't exhaust me; news of my parents divorcing made me realize that life was a circus; but now I felt like a lump of clay on this miserable day not because I was drained, but because I lost the seed of my life. I could no longer connect to my only friend Xander, who changed the melancholy of my thoughts and wishes into feathers of hope. I realized again that I was a helpless 12-year-old kid, and poems do not live; if I just had one more chance to fix it, I would risk my dreams for it.

While I was sitting and sobbing near the big pond, cursing my fate for giving me a stepmother with a heart of stone, my ears could hear footsteps approaching, but I didn't care because I knew it wasn't Xander. In my bluest hours, he showed me light and tuned my heart to the melody of life. It was the best of times, it was the funniest time, it was the worst of times, it was learning time, it was the craziest time, it was thoughtless time, it was fearless time, it was a hopeful time, it was the brightest time, it was the scariest time, it was playful time.

"Oliver, Oliver ... we have been searching for you everywhere. The ring ceremony is going to start. You have to be there to protect us from that monster stepmother," said Noah, panting for breath after running down the hills to reach our fishing pond, where we no longer went for fishing. Suddenly we had turned eggetarian as eggs couldn't walk and talk.

"Yes, Oliver. You must save us and bring our mother home. She left to live with Grandpa and Grandma on the other end of the green hills. Who will cook lip-smacking food? Who will comb my hair? Who will prepare our bed? Who will tell us stories? With whom will we play? How will we grow food? Can Mom live with us? Will she love us the same way?" And the list went on for Olivia as if I knew the answers.

"Stop bothering me. I don't want to be there. Xander is missing since morning."

"You won't be coming with us because your three-eared and five-legged plastic rabbit toy is missing. Come on, Noah, as Oliver also doesn't love us. He left us alone in this miserable hour," said my 7-year-old sister, Olivia, which shook me within and called out to my leftover courage to continue the fight. It was time for John Hancock to sign. I stood up and wiped off my tears, reminding myself of the promise I made to my loved ones with no fear, as my friend Xander was nearby. But now I couldn't turn back my ears to their flooding tears because of my fears. I turned and held my siblings' hands with an unspoken promise of never letting it go. I could see a tiny smile at the end of their lips, though what they needed were a strong back and muscular arms, but a slap of time had thrown us flat on the ground with no toys to play around with.

"How can I leave you both? I am coming along, and ..." I felt words choking in my throat, giving me no space to play around.

We started climbing the green hills across the meadows, listening to the chirps and whistling that pondered my heart, reminding me of the melodious times.

"Do you remember how we hid Mr. Peter's mushroom and told him that the white-crowned sparrow ate it all? He pleaded with us to tell him where to find those mushrooms in exchange for pancakes, and we sent him here to pluck these wild mushrooms. He cooked them with great culinary complexity only to cause red rashes all over Ms. Hannah's body, freaking her out and making her scream for hours," reminded Olivia, and tears rolled down my eyes as Xander had laid down the plan as usual, assigning it to me to work it out. Instead of a backbencher, he had made me the ringleader of our little circus here. The pain had started diminishing with each laughter that he bought for us.

"That was nothing. Do you remember when she first visited our farm animals and poultry? Mack almost chased her out with his narrow straight but ferocious horns until she fell into the swamp in Beck's sty. She babbled in her fancy Italian language, cursing us for the mess which we never accepted. Oliver, you did a great job," said Noah, and I smiled thinking about how I had fed Mack green chili with grass just before Hannah entered his community loafing shed. This hilarious prank was suggested by no other than Xander. After Mack started to chase Hannah, others followed him, and even Dad got scared and ran out. We were hiding behind the haystack, watching all this with our mouths shut, with our hands to contain our laughter. The subsequent weekend she didn't even fetch eggs from the poultry to impress Dad with her fake country girl image. I never believed that a young lady wearing spike heels stepping on our cowboy boots discussing a business proposal with my dad for converting our family mansion into an expensive resort could be trusted. Her five-weekday business trip soon converted to weekend leisure with a work trip. Her poppy red lipstick and sunglasses coordinated with fancy attire couldn't hide her toting desire to break my home.

The first day when mom saw her planting a kiss on my dad's cheek, she raised an alarm and fought with him, which was unusual as the earlier fight was over his laziness and drinking.

Mom worked hard to look after our farm as well as the vineyard. The vineyard belonged to her parents, and she, being the only child, was the sole owner of that huge property. She sent one-tenth of the money she earned from the vineyard to her parents Bob and Marilla. This often infuriated my dad, and those nights he spent in a nearby bar from where his mother dragged him home. This new chapter of Hannah in his life had turned our world upside down. Mom didn't want to move out with us, leaving this mansion in the hands of that succubus after working her butt off in raising the three of us along with our farm animals, not even leaving my complaining grandmother Victoria behind. Grandfather Henry was a very caring and accommodating person. His tutoring abilities never created a need for a tutor to teach us. He had amazing ways to teach literature, art, science, and humanity. Mathematics was at his wit's end because we always snoozed while solving problems, making his task of motivation taller, but he never gave up on his grandchildren.

"Mom left this morning to stay with Bob and Marilla. I was crying when Noah reminded me that you can fix things, and since then, we have been looking for you in the woods, farms, and fields. We didn't expect you to be here at this time of the day as you usually come here in the morning to feed the fishes," said Olivia affectionately, giving me a warm sisterly feeling to reduce my agony, which no free-wheeling back-seater could understand. Her words gave me hope in this hopelessness, and I refused to let go of her sweaty shaky hands.

She browsed me, saying, "I know you can do it. We will bring Mother home," and I couldn't say, "I can't make the magic work without Xander, my 4-foot-tall friend who wore half-pants and a bowtie."

When Xander was around, I could talk to animals and birds. They used to approach me with their long list of complaints for each other. Lily, the mother quail, came complaining about Baldy, the bald eagle, for stealing eggs from her nest. Since that day, their territories had been marked. No bird or animal would prey in our area, where all lived in harmony. Gabriel, the golden eagle, was elected to be their president and looked after their interests, which decreased my burden of feeding, playing, and sheltering them. Whenever Hannah sat in our beautiful kitchen garden, my tiny birdies used to fly around, pooping all over her. She started sitting there with an umbrella when my hummingbird Casper made holes all over, making her stomp her feet. One day she spotted me talking to Xander but couldn't see him, so she declared that I was as mad as a cornered rat. Yes, that's what she thought of us 'church rats,' fighting for food and plastic toys. We fought over food, snatching from each other's plates whenever mom made pancakes or pudding to express our love for one another. But a greedy poker-faced lady would never understand what family and togetherness mean. Now she was there in my home, organizing an expensive ring ceremony with my father to move in with us after throwing my mother out of his life. My faint little heart again began to sob, refusing to accept this as our future. Xander had almost fixed things when I unexpectedly lost him. I had turned the whole mansion upside down looking for my treasurable tiny plastic toy, which somewhat resembled our farm rabbits with whom he played. Whenever I was upset or angry, he came to my rescue. An average timid boy had turned to a new leaf to outrageously bomb Hannah's plan of overtaking his home. How could he let that happen? A fortunate night ago, she brought along a handy assistant who she claimed to be her niece. This 8-year-old girl Juniper was no titmouse, and she had her own tricks to make our lives miserable. Our every trick had to go through a counter trick, which landed us on this bad day.

In the past when Hannah hadn't jeopardized our lives, it used to be simple. In the vast acres of our land and a historic mansion, what kept me busy was the pond where I found Xander lying hidden between the mushy thick grasses after Hannah invaded my home. Somehow the rustling of woods and chirping of birds woke me up early in the morning, and I ran into the woods trying to catch my breath full of fresh air and fragrance. Homeschooling had its fun side of no timeline. So, before our governess Anna came, I ran down the green hills and woods racing for the pond to catch fish early for mom to cook it for lunch. My running started at 5 am and finished with playing games with my siblings Olivia and Noah when the sun was high in the sky. Always arriving late for breakfast made us an easy target for our mother's anger as she had to go to work. Sometimes she used to assign the task of serving food to Anna, who was very gentle with us. Although her heavy weight and aging body didn't lessen her burden, and we sometimes took pity on her and helped her with cleaning our animals and poultry and helped her in feeding and milking them, and still our grandmother never failed to criticize us whenever our father returned from work. He got furious with her false accusations of hiding her glasses or not fetching her water or making her room dirty to make us clean or disconnecting her television while she slept, and her creativity in this had no boundaries. When she first noticed Hannah and her son together, a devilish plot occupied her mind to bring her home and throw our mother out. Maybe her hatred for my mother showed upon us.

"You will be surprised to know that Grandmother Victoria was not letting our mother leave today morning. She is also crying, and grandfather is, as usual, sad over Mom's plight. I miss her already," said Olivia sadly, and I couldn't have felt more wretched about all this.

"Grandmother had a change of heart after she slipped down the stairway while coming to the hallway to step out for her usual late morning walk. This happened after she objected to Hannah's plan of an elaborate engagement ceremony without my parents' divorce legally. She had underestimated Hannah's ambition and cruelty. When she slipped, instead of calling a doctor, Hannah took her to the veterinarian who treated our horses, pigs, goats, sheep, and cattle and forced him to inject her with a syringe and medicine used to calm wild horses, and our grandmother didn't speak for days of her ordeal. When she came to her senses, it was too late for anything. My father, who was completely blinded by her charm and persuasively convincing attitude, failed to notice the plight of his parents.

Hannah, who had graced the magazine's cover page for all the wrong reasons, never failed to proudly recount those incidents to my father. He took great pleasure in listening to her stories. I wondered if those incidents truly happened, or if she deliberately orchestrated them, much like my grandmother's fall. Recently, her dog was found sleeping in her neighbour's house after being stolen by them. But Hannah's dog, Vector, informed me that Hannah had induced him with an oxytocin hormone just before her assistant, Ugandan, broke into her neighbour's house and added sleeping pills to Nancy's drink. She hid behind the curtains and waited for Nancy to sleep. Then she unclothed her before letting me lose. She left me there and called the reporters at four in the morning, informing them that somebody in Hannah's neighbourhood had stolen her dog. The reporters started checking the neighbourhood for this news on their cover page about a millionaire beauty losing her dog. I was horrified by Vector's revelation and refused to believe it, but he showed me the video which Ugandan had made while framing Nancy and showing an intimate scene with her. The video was intended for Hannah's ex-boyfriend, Liam, who broke up with her due to her reckless and insensitive behavior. To my disbelief, the video went viral on the internet, and Hannah turned it into a hilarious meme. As a result, Liam broke up with Nancy over it. I had shown the video to Dad, and Hannah cunningly shifted the blame onto her rival wellness brand, claiming they attempted to malign her. My place in my dad's eye fell more and he agreed to her demand of sending all three of us to a boarding school to learn some sense. She had completely side-lined my mom by then. The most kind-hearted and hardworking woman who never cared for herself in meeting our needs meant nothing to my dad as he was captivated by Hannah's youthful beauty and shiny coins. All these incidents were live before my eyes.

The day I saw Dad staring into Hannah's eyes with acceptance and appreciation, I had tried to warn Mom, but it was difficult to persuade her against her belief in her ruthless husband. She had closed her eyes to her miseries for us, and I couldn't take it anymore. That evening when I was crying near the pond, I noticed a small unidentified funny plastic toy which somewhat resembled a rabbit lying unattended on the grass. Its penetrating eyes and sweet smile forced me to pick it up and bring that harmless toy home and keep it on my shelf without realizing that it would become part of my life. That night at the dinner table, my mother objected to Hannah's closeness to her husband, which was silenced by my grandmother. I went to bed holding my new toy soaked with my tears. When I woke up in the morning,

Xander had cleaned my messy room and finished my homework. He was standing near my bed holding my favourite chocolate drink with marshmallow toppings. I opened my eyes and freaked out. The moment I opened my mouth to shout, he closed it with his furry lemon-yellow paws. I thought I was daydreaming or maybe I was in Alice's wonderland struggling to get out of the nightmare. Noah and Olivia barged into my room dancing. They were happy because, after a bad night, our mother had kept our favourite drink in our rooms. Olivia was still licking her glass of drink. I was surprised because Mom never gave us sugary drinks as the first thing in the morning. I finished my drink thinking Xander was my imagination and ran towards the kitchen to thank Mom. To my surprise, she was crying, and she told me that she had not cooked anything for anyone. I didn't mention the drink to her and ran wildly back to my room and found Xander looking outside my window.

"I love these woods. I have an old connection with it," he said feeling the winds which were fanning his furry dense hairs. His eyes shined like crystal, and his style was like a prince.

"Who are you?"

"I am Xander, the prince of Caledonia," he replied.

"Does everyone look like you in your kingdom?"

"Mostly, but like you humans, males and females have dissimilarities given by God. We help kids who are sad in this world," he replied.

"Is there any other parallel world other than yours?"

"You ask too many questions. Here you go," he said and handed me a catapult.

I gave him a confused look, prompting him to say, "There is your target. Close your eyes and aim at it."

I peeped outside and saw Hannah sitting there with my dad, holding his hand while kissing him with tea in her teacup and holding it in her other hand. With rage in my eyes, without a second thought, I aimed the tiny marble. She screamed when the hot tea spilled all over her thin night suit, making her in pain. My dad jumped up to help her. I became frantic as he never cared to wipe out my mom's tears. What mattered to him was that we, his parents, and his business were fine. I again aimed to hit Hannah, but Xander stopped me, saying, "Aggression is the killer. Patience and humbleness win," which seemed more like a mockery than reality as these inbuilt qualities didn't bring any happiness to my mother.

I slowly calmed myself and went to see my mother in the kitchen. I saw father running with a bucket of water, leaving my mother behind. Xander signaled me to take my mother there and let her help Hannah. I did that, but Hannah started shouting at my mother, saying that she threw a stone to break her cup. My dad believed her, and that increased my aggression. Xander stood there watching everything. The next events that we planned were carefully arranged to keep my mother out of the scene. Hannah got mild burns, which also gave her the opportunity to extend her stay with us. Every morning she woke up screaming with some giant bugs in her bed, who came out laughing after scaring her. By the time Dad came there, the bugs weren't there. He thought that because of the trauma of the burn, she was visualizing things. Vector played an important role in leaving her door slightly ajar. This gave her an excuse for not eating the right diet food, so she called her butler to stay in my home and cook for her. Slowly Dad started eating the fancy food cooked by Peter, and we had to break this chain. After Peter cooked food and decorated it to serve, we added a bit of naughtiness to it. Once when Hannah picked up a fresh cherry topping and took a sensuous bite, a worm came crawling out and waved at her. She threw all the food around and started jumping with fright. Since that day she has never touched any cherry. Seeing the smile on our faces, she understood that things were fishy, and so she called Juniper to stay with us. Ever since then, we had to face challenges too.

I still clearly remember the day when she bathed her cat in Noah's washroom when we went to the pond to play. Noah went to his washroom and sat in the bathtub, which was already prepared. He assumed that Mom or Anna might have done it, and he soaked himself in it to relax. The tub had slime and glue in it. His hair got glued, and he had to shave it off. He cried the whole day, but nobody said a word to Juniper, who winked at us and showed fake sympathy. To take revenge, we placed our friend Frankie, a giant python, in her bed. She slept the entire night curdling him and started to cry with the first rays of light. Hannah came running to her room and saw Frankie crawl out of her balcony door. Instead of pacifying her niece, she joined her in the screech. We laughed to our hearts' content, and after this, Juniper never played a prank.

We insisted Dad go for a camping trip as usual, but this time my mom stayed behind. Xander came along and slept in my tent. Noah and Olivia slept with Anna. Thankfully Juniper was scared to sleep alone, so Hannah gave her company. The best part was when Dad had to share his tent with Peter snoring all night because we slid out of one tent on our way. To make this camping trip adventurous, we sprinkled honey near Hannah's side, sparing Juniper this time. At around 3 am, Hannah started screaming and ran out of the tent, jumping into the cold lake water. Juniper woke up and saw ants crawling around. She also came running out of her tent and gave us an angry glance. We smiled at her while Xander cleaned our mess. As usual, we didn't take ownership of this chaos and had to pack our bags to go home. All the way, we were sad, but there was a feeling of satisfaction on seeing Hannah shiver with cold. The next few days, she was down with a cold and had to drink hot chilly soup.

Our struggle didn't end here. She was not the kind of woman who would give up easily. But one morning, what took us by surprise was when Juniper came to talk with tears in her eyes. I wondered what she was hiding behind those beautiful blue eyes. "Will you let me come over after my aunt marries your dad?" she said, and my ship of hope sank.

"Are you crazy? Why will my dad marry your aunt?"

"I heard them talking about their engagement after fifteen days. Your dad has already filed for divorce. He is not ready to give a penny of compensation to your mom. If she asks for it, he will send you all with her," she replied, and I felt like screaming out loud. Xander heard it with tears in his eyes and walked down the stairs to see my mom. I ran behind him and dragged him into the woods to talk things out.

"Why can't you use magic on Hannah and throw her out of our lives?"

"I can't do that. How will you learn to fight for what is right?" he said unhappily.

I left him standing alone there and didn't realize that I would not see him for long. In anger, I never called him. Mom had moved into the attic to be with us. She was adamant about not moving out and refused to accept that her husband had filed for divorce to marry a deflated tire. That's what I thought of Hannah. A beautifully decorated flat tire. My mom was still beautiful but didn't care about her gifted beauty much. So, one morning I insisted she take a bath in the fragrant aroma water that I had prepared. Anna gave her a relaxing aromatic massage, which brought out the natural glow of her skin, and I bought her a beautiful dress with my pocket money. My mom that day looked like a queen, and my father was gobsmacked on seeing his wife as if he was noticing her for the second time. Unexpectedly, my mom's childhood friend paid a visit to her after thirteen years. He had proposed to Mom, but she was forced to choose Dad as he had a mansion and farms. Now he was a silver fox and yet single. This somewhat made my dad jealous, but Hannah didn't let it last long. He invited us over for dinner at his fancy hotel in town. Anna had stitched an elegant gown for Mom, and she wore it for dinner. Dad somewhat changed his mind and came along. But Hannah couldn't take it and abruptly interrupted the dinner with her friends, who humiliated my mother in public. Dad got angry with Hannah for the first time, which hurt her, and she shouted that he had already filed for divorce. She even went ahead and announced the engagement date. Mom started to sob lightly and to hide her pain further she dressed it up with a fake smile. Mr. Kenneth, being a gentleman, came down on his knees and handed Mom a tissue to wipe out her tears. He said, “It’s not late Katie. I am still waiting for you.”

Hearing those words, my dad left, but I was happy to see his anger. Somewhere he still loved Mom then why was he getting engaged to Hannah? That night I went to speak to grandfather about it, who was equally disturbed, but he promised to talk to Dad. Last night he informed me that Dad has made up his mind as she is wealthy and can take his business to new heights. I thought about Mr. Kenneth’s proposal to my mom and admired her for resisting it.

With all these thoughts replying in my mind, I didn’t realize that I had reached my mansion which didn’t feel like home. We all were sobbing when a loud commotion was heard on the lawn. We ran towards the lawn thinking that Mom might be there fighting with Dad. I didn’t want her to do it anymore. Not even for us. But when we reached there, the situation was contrary to our expectations. Dad and Hannah were fighting. Dad was throwing things around and shouting at her. Juniper came running to me and gave me my Xander. I looked at her with surprise and she said, “My mom Hannah had kept it in her cupboard. I had seen her sneaking into your room a few days ago.”

“How could you lie to me Juniper that Hannah is your mother?”

“I too came to know it just now," and pointed towards a handsome middle-aged man and said, "He is my biological dad, and my mom had taken millions of dollars from him to hide the truth. He is now divorced and didn’t want to miss this opportunity of ruining Hannah’s life as she did. I will be living with him. I am happy that your friend Xander helped me.”

She stepped forward and kissed my cheeks, making my siblings blush. “Will you be my boyfriend, Oliver?” she asked, and I nodded, saying, “But you will have to promise me that you will spend all your summers here with us.”

Juniper jumped with delight and hugged me while her dad stepped forward and welcomed me to their home. My tears fell on Xander, and he patted my back, saying, "Who says magic doesn't happen?"

Dad ran towards his car to bring Mom home, but he didn't expect that she would have her conditions laid before coming back. Technically, Dad agreed and made his wife a partner for everything in his life. A month later, Mom signed a contract with Mr. Kenneth to turn half-part of the mansion into a holiday home for families. Our business reached new heights, and Mom was on the cover page of many magazines for all the right reasons. Juniper came to spend her next summer with us and then the next and so on until one day I had grown enough to propose her to be my love for life. Xander sometimes visited us, taking leave from his responsibility of helping kids. Noah and Olivia also came along. Our little happy family was increasing year by year, and I had never daydreamed of this any year. My parents grew old together, and my dad never let go of my mother again. Mr. Kenneth had married a fine woman approved by my mother, and they were blessed with two kids. We all often met for dinner and Christmas while Hannah was still alone somewhere not known to any of us. I was thankful to Dad for accepting Juniper as a part of our family, and he never mentioned her mother. She was very close to my mom. Sometimes life gives you more than you want not because magic is there, but because you refuse to give up on your dreams. I held my 5-year-old son's hand and gave him Xander, saying, "When you are sad, don't be mad. Hold him tight to show you light."

He looked at me and asked, "Are you going somewhere?" and I replied, "Nowhere."

MY 19TH HALLOWEEN

The agony of missing my love was deeper than Enceladus' Ocean with my methane feeling trapped between them.

6:30 am - Stop ringing and let me sleep.

6:45 am - Oh! God, can't live with this heaviness. Why didn't I take his address? Where can I find him? Sam left without saying a word. Why did I ignore him after his confession about Samantha? I want to meet him once again. Give me strength.

7:00 am - Wake up, Salma. Breakfast is ready.

7:10 am - Why don't I feel like going to school? It's been thirty days since I have seen him. Why did I shrug at him for choosing Samantha? They had been dating for a couple of months. I was the intruder. Rather than dying of heartache, we could have been friends.

7:20 am - Mom, I am going.

7:21 am - Are you ready to marry Salman? He is coming for dinner on the fifth of next month.

7:22 am - Mom, don't bother me. I am going to school.

7:23 am - Seriously school? It's Halloween today.

I realized that I had lost track of time. My weekend date with coffee had brought me closer to my server Sam. His funny puns with hot brewing coffee topped with cream always made my day. Between a couple of Sundays, I and coffee became inseparable.

7:25 am - I am going to the café down the street.

7:26 am - Again going there. What's wrong with you?

7:27 am - Drinking chocolate is not wrong.

7:40 am - Hey! Where have you been?

I could hear my heartbeat. I turned to look at that perfect sleek spotless face which now was covered with pimples. But this didn't move my eyes away.

7:41 am - I...I was busy with my art project. How is Samantha?

7:42 am - She is happy with Adam. You relax, my love, till I get your favourite coffee.

7:43 am - Oh! God. How couldn't I see it coming? This is why they were arguing when I last came here. Sam called me his love. Thank you, God. Soon he will be mine.

Suddenly my gloomy morning turned bright with sunshine, and I was rocking on my fancy chair.

7:50 am - Here comes your favourite coffee. I hope I haven't lost touch.

7:51 am - Where do you live?

7:52 am - In that house across the streets. My landlady doesn't like visitors, so I don't bring chicks home.

7:53 am - Thanks for the coffee.

8:30 am - Will you not invite me for Halloween tonight?

8:31 am - Celebrating it alone in my room.

8:45 am - Mom, I am home. Dad is not around, so let's celebrate Halloween tonight. I am going to buy decorations.

6:50 pm - Mom, I am going to invite a friend who lives across the street.

6:51 pm - You can't invite a boy.

6:52 pm - Too late, Mom.

7:05 pm - Happy Halloween Mrs. Jolie. I am here to invite Sam to a Halloween party tonight. Can I see him in his room?

7:06 pm - Are you sure you are here to meet my nephew Sam because he died a month ago?

7:07 pm - I am sure my Sam is not your nephew.

7:08 pm - Does your Sam own a café?

7:09 pm - Yes.

7.10 pm - Unfortunately, we are referring to the same Sam.

7:11 pm - I can see you are old and can forget facts. Sam is alive and I drank coffee in his café today morning.

7:12 pm - Are you crazy? Come with me and see for yourself that the café is closed.

7:13 pm - Sam might have gone somewhere closing his shop. I am sure he will come back. Please tell him that I have invited him to my house across the street for a Halloween party.

7:15 pm - You are an impossible girl.

7:30 pm - Mom, have you made cookies and cake? My friends might come any minute.

8:30 pm - Who is that special one, Salma? You have not stopped looking at the door.

8:31 pm - His name is Sam, and I really like him, Claire.

8:34 pm - I also want to meet your mystery date. But let's watch the Annabelle movie. Halloween without horror is like pumpkin pie without pumpkin spice.

9:30 pm - Claire, I am going to check who is at the door.

9:35 pm - Mom, did you order pizza? Someone delivered it to our door.

9:36 pm - Maybe your dad might have ordered it. I informed him about the party. Initially, he was angry, but then the heat went down.

9:37 pm - Mom, you are impossible.

9:40 pm - Come on, guys. Dad ordered pizza for us. Surprisingly, no name is there on the box, but I am sure it will taste great.

9:45 pm - What happened, Claire? Why are you eating pizza as if tasted a worm?

9:46 pm - Claire, its flavor and texture remind me of a very familiar café. I feel someone ghosted me. I love this pizza.

9:47 pm - Stop being a food inspector and just gobble it.

9:48 pm - Sparkle is right, Salma. Don't be a show spoiler.

10:10 pm - Sam hasn't come yet.

10:11 pm - Salma, don't be sad. It is quite possible that the old lady forgot to convey your message to Sam.

10:15 pm - Aunt Sofia, the party was great. We are here to say goodbye as it's late, and we must go home.

10:16 pm - Thank you, girls, for coming. Goodnight.

10:20 pm - Mom, I am going to bed.

11:45 pm - Sam, why didn't you come for the Halloween party? I am angry with you. I organized this for you.

11:50 pm - I can't come to any of your parties, Salma. I know how you feel about me, but I realized it late. Your café keys are on the right side of my drawer along with the transfer certificate. I have faith in you. Please take care of my aunt. She is very old and has nobody to look after. I must go.

11:59 pm - Sam, please don't go. I love you and will never let go of you.

12:00 pm - Salma, why are you screaming? Wake up.

12:01 pm - Mom, I had a nightmare. Can you take me to see Mrs. Jolie?

12:02 pm - We will go in the morning, Salma.

12:03 pm - Mom, now. Please.

12:04 pm - Don't cry like this. I am getting worried about you. Is it about some boy?

12:05 pm - Mom, let's go. I feel Sam is in danger. I must help him.

12:07 pm - Who is Sam?

12:10 pm - He is the owner of the café that I used to go to every Saturday.

12:12 pm - Don't tell me that you are dating him.

12:15 pm - Mom, I am not dating anyone. Will you come along, or should I go alone?

12:16 pm - Is it far?

12:20 pm - No.

12:35 pm - I am sorry to bother you at midnight, Mrs. Jolie. I want Sam's room keys.

12:40 pm - Mom, this is Sam's café keys and papers.

12:45 pm - I am sorry for Sam, my child. Don't cry.

1:15 pm - I am grieving, mom. Salman will have to wait for a few years.

Two months later, just before New Year.

4:30 pm - Mrs. Isabella's cat died today. She didn't know how Sophie died suddenly.

4:32 pm - Did she report the case?

4:33 pm - Will ask her tomorrow after the burial.

31st December 2019

10:30 am - I came to know that today morning Mrs. Olivia's pet dog died. Everyone is taken aback because both pets were healthy.

10:32 am - I am going to the animal shelter to see that all animals are doing fine.

12:30 pm - Are all animals in the shelter fine?

12:31 pm - Yes, Mom, but while crossing the area near the lake, I found birds and animals dead.

12:32 pm - How is it possible? There has never been any incidence of mass death of animals near the lake before.

12:34 pm - You are right, Mom. Emma's dad, who works in the nearby pharmaceutical company, is also sick. Surprisingly, his peers are also sick.

12:35 pm - They are having difficulty breathing, and they are vomiting.

12:36 pm - Olivia and Isabella's pets had the same symptoms.

12:37 pm - I am going to the municipal to inform the authorities about dead animals near the lake and similar symptoms of animals and humans.

4:30 pm - Why are you sleeping on the sofa, Mom?

4:32 pm - Mom, what's wrong? You are shivering and sweating at the same time. Let me call 911 for help.

4:35 pm - I called for help and informed them that the disease might be infectious, so they should take proper precautions before coming here. Mom, why aren't you speaking?

5:00 pm - Your mom is dead.

5:01 pm - She was just shivering. How can she be dead?

5:02 pm - She also suffered cardiac arrest. We are taking the body for autopsy.

5:10 pm - I am also shivering.

5th January 2020

1:00 pm - Hello, Nurse. Why am I in the hospital?

1:02 pm - We saved you from cardiac arrest like your mother.

1:03 pm - I am 19. How can I have a cardiac arrest like my mother?

1:04 pm - Your complete locality has been sealed. People have been put under quarantine. Cases are rising every minute, and the hospital is full of patients. There are two types of this infection. One is like yours, and the second is breathlessness and vomiting resulting in death.

1:08 pm - Anybody knows why it is happening?

1:10 pm - Not yet.

1:15 pm - Has the pharmaceutical factory been inspected?

1:16 pm - Why do you suspect the factory?

1:17 pm - While I was crossing the lake to visit the animal shelter, the smell due to dead animals and the sound of commotion from the factory was very disturbing. I know you are the new mayor of this town. You have the authority to inspect it.

1:18 pm - Thanks for the information.

7th January 2020

8:00 am - Your information saved the town.

8:01 am - How, Abigail?

8:02 am - You have been cured, and your blood sample has been sent for analysis and study. Fifty people are dead, and everyone is wondering how you survived.

My mind spoke the word "Sam," and I felt he was standing beside me.

8:03 am - In that factory, they were making viruses as bioweapons which were to be sold to our enemies. Due to an employee's carelessness, it got leaked and contaminated the environment. Lives have been lost, and all the nearby areas have been vacated, but containing the spread via air is difficult. Your blood sample gave us a clue for the cure but still, containment is a challenge. God! Save humanity.

8:04 am - Your immune response was incredible as you had been bitten by a dog. The germ that entered your body triggered this unexpected response.

8:05 am - I hope humanity finds the cure and containment.

I saw my mother standing beside me, smiling, and tears were flowing down my cheeks.

8:10 am - Do you know that young handsome mayor?

8:11 am - He is a patron of my coffee shop.

8:12 am - I think he has a thing for you.

I looked silently towards my mom and Sam. They were smiling at me as if giving their approval.

8:15 am - What are you staring at? I can't see anything outside your window.

8:16 am - Don't you feel somebody wanted to save humanity and deliberately leaked the virus without anticipating the consequences.

8:20 am - Who wants to lose their job and go to prison?

8:21 am - A person who loves humanity more than himself.

After a long pause.

8:30 am - In 2-3 days, you will be able to stand and walk. You need not wear PPE safety equipment or complete head-covered masks because viruses cannot infect you again.

8:35 am - Can I join here as a trainee nurse to help patients?

8:37 am - Why not? That's very thoughtful of you. But after a few days because you are still weak and might not be able to handle the pressure.

8:40 am - How about 21st January?

8:41 am - Sounds good, but be kind to yourself also.

I glanced at the calendar and had never felt so content.

Next Number

It was raining heavily, and Alisha was, as usual, sipping black coffee. The rain droplets falling on the clinic's window felt as hollow as she was feeling. Listening to her patients' plights had kept her marriage going, although it had hit a rough patch a long time ago. Marrying her sweetheart at the tender age of twenty-three had turned her world upside down in five years. Being a homeopath and an emotional counselor was not easy for her. Women came for counseling every day to her clinic. Wiping their tears and making them feel emotionally secure was like her daily routine that she followed religiously. Her job meant more than anything to her. After five years of her marriage, she was still barren. Ashok was not yet prepared for a child in their busy life. Their hectic schedule always kept them on their toes, leaving very little time for each other. Her beautiful brown eyes had thick droplets of tears in them.

Her first meeting with Ashok was fresh in her mind. It was raining heavily when she got off the college bus, and her umbrella broke while she tried to open it. She was visiting her friend Amrita to attend the marriage of Amrita's elder sister Anshul. While she was busy trying to fix it somehow, the heavy rain drenched her completely. Ashok moved forward to cover her under his big black umbrella, which was enough for both. It was again 15th July, but 2019; five long years with Ashok did not fly away, and she had to live each day hiding tears in her eyes. Born and brought up in the small town of Mirzapur and moving to Prayagraj to study homeopathy was not easy for her. Soon her parents also shifted to Prayagraj. She touched one droplet of water from inside but only felt coldness, as if her feelings were cold. If the tea was hotter, then Ashok would throw it, sometimes spilling it on her, making her scream. If food had more salt, he would leave it, screaming that her parents didn't teach her anything. The ordeal didn't end there. In bed, if she was not hot, he would remind her of all his girlfriends who were so hot in bed, making Alisha feel even more miserable about herself.

But with her family, Ashok was very caring and loving. Last year her father underwent bypass surgery. The battery fitted in her father's heart never gave Alisha the courage to walk out of Ashok's life. This had increased her difficulties. Her clinic was full of female patients. There were hardly any men who came for emotional counseling. She somewhat believed that this new generation of men lacked emotion.

"Madam! Can I send in the next patient?" asked Sanskriti, peeping from behind the door.

"In five minutes, Sanskriti," replied Alisha, trying to hide her teary eyes.

"Charlotte is here. She is with her two-year-old son and wants to see you soon as she must pick up her daughter from dance class," Sanskriti continued, trying to ignore the tears in Alisha's eyes.

"Send her," said Alisha while dabbing her eyes with a tissue to absorb her pain, but it was still inside her and not on the tissue.

There was silence, and Alisha again sat on the revolving chair, which she sometimes turned to avoid the patient's tears by looking at the curtains and swallowing her own tears. She would empower and help them, and today she needed help and empowerment.

"Good evening, Doctor," said Charlotte, hurriedly putting her son in the play area and coming to sit on the patient's chair.

"You look much content and happy. Tell me every bit of it."

"I followed your advice; I have put my daughter in dance class, and I have started teaching French in a play school. Ranjit is much more caring and loving after all this. He even spoke of marrying me after this Australia trip. Indian cricketers are in high demand, and he is at the peak of his career right now. I had told him that I would return to my country, leaving both my kids behind. He answered me that he will fix things. He will lose some of his female fan following if he marries me, but he is ready to pay the price," said Charlotte in a bubbly mood.

Alisha faintly smiled and said, "So what is the problem now?"

"My mother, she wants us to return to France and marry a French man," replied Charlotte with tears.

"What do you want?"

"I too feel the same. At least we will have our relatives. My childhood friend got divorced and has two kids. I can move to France with my mother and both kids and live in the countryside home with her. Albert also lives nearby. We might get a chance to date each other, and if things are fine, then marry him," she replied while feeling uncomfortable.

"Don't worry. Ranjit will not come to know anything. Are you talking to your childhood friend?"

There was silence, and she knew her answer.

"Will Ranjit allow you to take his kids with you? Will Sam and Sammy leave their father? Will you be able to forgive yourself for leaving both of your kids behind?"

"I am not sure," she said. Alisha lost her cool and said, "you are only thinking about yourself. When everything is in your favor, you are running away leaving all your happiness behind for some uncertain childhood friend. Do you really think you will be fine?"

Charlotte sobbed lightly and said, "I was wrong. I can't leave my world behind when everything is falling into place. I am not going to France."

"Good decision, and take your medicines on time."

"Alisha, I knew I can always count on you," said Charlotte, wiping away her tears and standing up to leave.

"Listen less to your mother's advice, Charlotte."

"Sure, I will do," said Charlotte and left the room with her son, Sam.

"Next patient."

"Hello, Alisha," said Leelavati, smiling brightly.

Alisha's sleek, perfect face with a sharp nose showed a smile line.

This was the most amazing thing about Alisha. She smiled and cried with her patients. They were not just numbers for her but real people with emotions. She treated them that way instead of just numbers. But it had been four years since she last laughed light-heartedly.

After dating Ashok for one year, they got married on 15th July 2015. Today, on her wedding anniversary, she sat there in her clinic, waiting for a call from Ashok. She still remembered how humbly he escorted her to Amrita's house. Ashok was Amrita's elder brother Gopal's friend. He had just started his practice under a senior neurosurgeon in Prayagraj. The doctor was like some president of some country there. Ashok was in the limelight with all the girls talking about him until Alisha came, who quickly became the spotlight of all the new young hearts.

Alisha checked her phone while managing a nod of approval for Leelavati.

"If you are busy, then I can come later," she said, turning to leave.

"Not at all. Just checking for my patients' messages if someone needs help," lied Alisha, showing her a chair to sit on.

"How is your son? Did he leave his wife for his girlfriend?"

"No. That witch seems to be drinking our blood. Where will Malini go with our seven-year-old granddaughter? I sometimes curse myself for giving birth to this Ravan. He has stopped talking to us also. We are his enemy. And if this was not enough, he has moved in with this twenty-year-old witch," said Leelavati without pause.

Alisha picked up her pen to jot down her statement, which was a problem for her and needed counseling.

"I am worried for my daughter-in-law and seven-year-old Nisha, who has started to smile less and ask often about her father. We are tired of lying that he is in the USA for work," she further added while Alisha noted a few points in her diary.

"Since when has he moved in with his girlfriend?"

"This is why you took my appointment stating an emergency."

"It's just two days. He will come back," said Alisha confidently, fixing her beautiful chiffon dupatta and fuller figure hidden beneath a loose kurta. The pink colour made her look like a pink goddess with moist eyes.

"You don't understand, Alisha. What if he divorces Malini and leaves his aging parents for that witch," said Leelavati, moving back and forth in her chair impatiently.

"What does Malini have to say about this?"

"She is adamant on her decision of not divorcing Mithilesh, but how long," replied Leelavati, stopping to a standstill.

"As long as you support her, I am sure your son Mithilesh will return home. Hold on to patience and find ways for him to meet his family. Be more gentle and polite with Malini. Encourage her to pursue a hobby or work if she wants."

"Work. She is not that educated. Malini's father is a police constable. We didn't want a working woman, so we chose Malini," replied Leelavati, observing what Alisha was noting down.

"What is she good at other than household chores?"

"She stitches beautifully, and her embroidery skill is extraordinary."

"Make her join a fashion designing class. Let her be independent. I am sure Mithilesh will again love and accept his family."

"You are right. Till date, you haven't given me any wrong advice. I am sure this will work," said Leelavati, applauding Alisha's suggestion.

"How old is Malini?"

"They have a ten-year age gap. Malini is twenty-six years old," replied Leelavati, surprised at her question.

"Did your son approve of this relationship during the time of their marriage?"

"Yes. But why?"

"I feel he was not looking for independent girls. What does his girlfriend do?"

"She is studying engineering," replied Leelavati angrily.

"Patience is the key. Please talk to Malini about my suggestion. I am sure the table will turn for her."

With a ray of hope, Leelavati stood up to leave.

"Your next session is not needed immediately. I am sure you will handle things. In case of anxiety, call me."

"Sure, I will," said Leelavati and walked outside, swaying her neatly tied hair.

"There are no more patients. Should I take a fresh appointment?" asked Sanskriti.

"No. Book a table for two in Taj. You can start to wind up."

Alisha picked up her phone to call Ashok, but he didn't answer. She typed, "Hey! I have booked a table for us in the Taj. Be there by 8 pm."

She then picked up her purse to leave. Just then her phone beeped. "Can't be there at 8 pm."

Her eyes were teary, and her mind drifted into the past. She remembered how he used to do everything for her before they entered wedlock. Was it just for show? Did he mean it?

Alisha sat there, thinking about how they met a few years ago.

"You look awesome in this lehenga," said Ashok and came a bit closer to her. She stepped behind and light-heartedly said, "Maintain your distance."

Amrita poked her lightly from behind and said, "Alisha, time to escort the bride to the stage. Let's go to her room. I don't want to miss my single double bedroom without my sister."

It was the sangeet and mehndi night. Ashok was following her everywhere like a magnet. They escorted Anshul to the stage for sangeet and mehndi. The ceremony started with Mehndi on Anshul's hands. Boys and girls danced at the sangeet. Party songs filled the air, and attendees had to speak at the top of their voices. Vaastu was looking at Alisha and was uncomfortable when Ashok came near her.

"I think you have two admirers," said Amrita in a hushed tone. Amrita had invited her batch to her sister's wedding. Vaastu also came to attend the wedding, but his secret crush on Alisha was revealed after Ashok started to follow Alisha everywhere. Alisha also secretly looked for Ashok when he wasn't near.

"What's cooking up, girl?" teased Amrita, and Alisha replied, "Not sure." Ashok invited Alisha on stage to dance to the latest beats of 2015. The pleasant spring season of March added to the captivating night. Early in the morning, Ashok and Vaastu had come to help Mahesh. Amrita teased her brother Mahesh for not choosing a girl for himself. Mahesh was too occupied in managing the party with hundreds of attendees. Ashok and Vaastu both were helping Mahesh arrange for the guests. Ashok went on his knees and asked for Alisha's hand to dance, while Vaastu watched with teary eyes. Alisha accepted, and they danced, least bothered about who all were watching them. Vaastu sat in a corner when Amrita called him on stage to dance, and he obliged. Somewhere, Amrita felt that Vaastu was a better match for Alisha due to her submissive and forgiving nature.

More guests joined the stage to dance, and in no time, everyone was moving with the rhythm. The next day was the marriage ceremony, and the groom's side had already arrived. They were also staying in the same hotel as the bride's family.

Ashok had already won Alisha's attention, and Vaastu was still longing for her attention. He decided to do something instead of watching their love story grow. But, not to his surprise, Ashok went on his knees and put a flower ring on Alisha's finger. The crowd cheered for them, and Vaastu stood there holding his broken heart. Alisha did not expect this sudden gesture from Ashok and stood there speechless. Amrita came near her and whispered in her ears. They suddenly left the stage and went to the terrace area.

"Vaastu is humbler and more caring. You have known him for five years. How can you say yes to someone whom you met five hours ago?" asked Amrita.

"I have not said yes to Ashok, I am also surprised but I think I can give him a chance."

"You are looking superficially. Maybe his kind gesture swept you off. He is not so kind. I am also surprised by his sudden liking for you. All his family members are doctors except his mother, but she educated both her children and they are doctors. Ashok is a neurosurgeon. Financially Vaastu is no match for him but other than this, Ashok is no match to Vaastu. You also know that I am right about them," convinced Amrita.

"I am not marrying anyone of them. This is my final year. I must pass with flying colours and start practicing."

"What are you girls doing here? The mocktail counter will be full soon. Grab your glasses before it gets crowded," said Mahesh from behind, and both smiled in agreement.

Mahesh hurriedly left while they decided to return to the hall to avoid eye contact and comments.

"I will give equal opportunities to both men."

"See that you don't drown sailing on two boats," remarked Amrita.

Alisha had earlier also come to Amrita's home. Both were close friends and shared the same room in the college hostel. Amrita was an average-built girl a little shorter than Alisha, who had height apt for modeling. Both friends came to the mocktail counter while touching their long black lustrous hair and gossiping.

"Mocktail for ladies," said Ashok and handed them a glass of mocktail.

"How did you know that we are going to the mocktail counter?" asked Amrita, surprised.

"I am a mind reader," joked Ashok without much discussion. They gulped it down and went to the stage again to dance.

This time Vaastu immediately grabbed Alisha's arms to dance, and Amrita joined them, and so did all their friends. The beautiful dance night was over, and everyone dispersed to meet for the final wedding day.

Alisha looked at her phone one last time hoping Ashok might have changed his mind. But there was no change in his plan.

"Sanskriti, please cancel the booking at Taj I have changed my mind," said Alisha packing her stuff to leave. She went down and started her car to go home. She wondered if it was home or a house with compassion and love missing.

Even with less traffic due to rain, the road seemed to be endless. She parked her car in the parking lot and went inside the lift. She saw a five-year-old girl and smiled at her. The little girl, who was eating chocolate, moved towards her mother as if Alisha would take her chocolate. Seeing her reaction, Alisha laughed. The ladies said hello, and the mother explained to her daughter that Alisha would not snatch her chocolate. The lift stopped on the second floor, and Alisha stepped out to unlock the door of her house. To her surprise, the door was already unlocked. She suspiciously went inside to see who was there, as her house help and Sanskriti also had duplicate keys for work. Ashok was not home so early, but to her surprise, she saw the house decorated, and pictures of them on the wall. While she was looking around, Ashok hugged her and wished her a happy wedding anniversary.

"You remembered this time."

"Sorry for forgetting last year," said Ashok while showing Alisha the decoration. She felt that she was dreaming. Ashok did this for her. She could not imagine as he had arranged the dining table and food was kept there, and a scented candle was lit.

"I will freshen up and come," said Alisha and left hurriedly.

Ashok got busy serving food on their plates, and soon Alisha joined.

Alisha didn't remember when they last ate together, but she was happy as well as stunned by the change in Ashok.

They made love later and woke up the next day for their usual routine. Alisha smiled when she woke up. Household chores were her department, and Ashok never helped her with it.

"I am preparing a sunshine omelet and bread toast with a glass of orange juice. Do you need anything else?"

"Why do you have to ask the same question every morning? I will eat whatever you make," replied Ashok.

Alisha knew that dream night was over, and he was the same Ashok. She served him breakfast and packed for herself. She went down and started her car to reach the clinic.

"Sanskriti, I left my patient register at home. It's kept on the bookshelf; can you please get it? Here are my home keys. Don't carry duplicate ones from the office," said Alisha, tossing a bunch of keys to Sanskriti.

"Sure," said Sanskriti and hurriedly left.

Patients were coming, and Alisha was waiting for Sanskriti to return with the register. She thought of starting the session as there was a lot of rush, and patients were losing patience. Alisha was wondering why it was taking so long for Sanskriti to arrive. She went out of the chamber to call the first patient.

"Shalini, please come," she said.

"Today Sanskriti hasn't come," said Shalini, making herself comfortable in a chair.

"You look tired. Do you need some water?" said Alisha, pouring two glasses of water for them.

"Thanks. I and Amit fought in the morning, and after that, I left for the clinic," said Shalini.

"Why did you fight? I told you not to fight, what was the argument about?" asked Alisha, looking around for a pen and paper to make a note of their discussion, so that next time she could refer.

Due to the large number of patients, it was difficult to remember everything.

"Who would cook breakfast?" replied Shalini, and Alisha sat with her hand on her head, unable to say anything.

"I knew it sounds weird, but it's a genuine problem. I have my early morning class, and he must leave for the office. Who will make breakfast? Amit is not happy with the idea of cooking as no men in his family cook. So, he refuses to do it," explained Shalini.

"Have you heard of cereal and milk, bread, juice, fruits, and cooking at night and refrigerating it? How can you fight because of food?"

"It's not about cooking. It's about sharing daily chores responsibility," defended Shalini.

"Is it more important than peace? Change comes slowly and doesn't happen overnight. On Sunday you can share the kitchen and cook something together for fun. Don't fight over it, keep a house help if needed."

"Flight is not just about food. He talks all day and night to one of his female colleagues over the excuse of office work. We hardly spend time together. I don't know what to do," said Shalini sadly.

"Talk it out, stick with him while he is talking. Don't leave the room. Read a book in the same room while he is chatting. If he is into you, he will notice it, and if not, then he will get angry. You will get your answer."

With a tearful voice, Shalini said, "Thanks for your advice."

"Shalini please send the next number while you leave."

"I will," said Shalini and left.

"Good morning, Mr. Mehra. Today you are early. Are you taking your medicine on time? Have you shifted with your son and daughter-in-law?"

"Nice to see you cheerful today. I find more darkness in your eyes than any of your patients. Call it age or experience, we old people have an eye on everything. I discarded all belongings of my wife to grieve. I feel she is with me, and I don't have to sleep with all her belongings to feel her presence. Thanks for your advice on the same. I want to tell you that you are a wonderful therapist, but your pain can be seen in your dark brown eyes. My daughter is your age, and I would advise her the same. Self-love is the key that you taught me. Then only you can love your family selflessly. You will know if they are sad and why they are sad. You can understand them better and love them without any reason. If you expect a lot, you get more pain in that relationship because your expectation was high from that relationship. It's not a barter system but it's about empathy and selfless giving. I did that, and this is why after my wife's demise I went into a state of shock. I had never imagined my life without her. My expectation was to see her always. I felt while grieving I neglected people who were with me. I didn't care how they felt when I stopped eating and drinking just holding my wife's picture. If it would not have been your counseling sessions I would have passed away. You gave me a new life. I want to live for my children. They love me and can't see me this way. My wife cannot return, but what she did I will do the same. Now I spend all my time with my grandchildren. I read them stories, bring them from school, play with them and I am living my childhood again with them," said Mr. Mehra.

"I am thrilled to hear changes and now I am sure you don't need a counseling session. You are perfect."

"In case of any difficulty can I reach you over the phone?" said Mr. Mehra.

"Why not? Also, you can......"

“I am back. Here is the file,” said Sanskriti hurriedly.

“Were you in a war zone? Why do you look as if you are struggling with someone?”

“I forgot my helmet while I was driving, so shabby hair and I forgot to iron my clothes in a hurry today,” replied Sanskriti placing the patient register on Alisha’s desk.

“See who is next.”

Sanskriti left to check the patient entry register.

Suddenly they heard a loud commotion. Sanskriti came running inside and said, “There is a man with a gun. In fact, four men with guns, I can see three more coming.”

“Call the police,” said Alisha while standing to go out, but before she could move, the four gunmen stepped inside and locked the door. Mr. Mehra stood up to negotiate, but they hinted him to sit quietly. They removed their masks and asked, “What did you instruct my sister? Where is she? Who was she dating? We are going kill both and you. How dare she agree to marry someone outside our community? Our father is the leader of our community. We will not tolerate this indecency.”

“Please listen to me. I have hundreds of patients coming. I don’t know whom you are referring to.”

In anger, one of them broke the glass vase and shouted, “You gave someone advice, and you don’t know who she is and which family she belongs to.”

“My job is to help patients, and I will never give any advice that will be harmful to my patients.”

“Her name is Amravati; she has eloped with her boyfriend. We are going to shoot both, and then it is your number. If you don’t want to die, then call her,” said one of them.

“Who are you?”

"I am her brother Swaroop, and these are my men," he replied.

Alisha scrolled through the patient register to call her.

"Hello," said a feeble voice.

"Amravati, you didn't come for your session. Why? It was due a week ago."

"I am not in Mumbai," she said.

"Did you run away with your boyfriend? It is in the newspaper," said Alisha.

"Yes, I did. My brother and father were not letting us marry. So, I eloped with my boyfriend. We have secretly tied the knot and are happy," replied Amravati sobbing lightly.

Sanskriti knocked on the door, and Alisha said, "She is my assistant. Please let her come inside."

The last man opened the door, and policemen pushed the door and nabbed them all.

"I am here for my sister. This woman advised her to elope," shouted Swaroop.

Policemen looked at Alisha, and she asked Amravati, "Did I advise you to elope with your boyfriend?"

"No. You told me to talk with my family. I did, but they slapped me and told me that if I marry that guy, both of us will die," replied Amravati.

"Sit in jail for troubling a medical practitioner," said Inspector Divakar.

"This woman is lying. My sister could be in danger," said Swaroop.

"This is why you came to kill all of us? Because she is in danger, or because she is safe, and you are in danger in her life."

"You cannot stop her from marrying anyone of her choice; there is the law. Also, you cannot carry a gun in someone's clinic and threaten them," said Inspector Divakar.

While Inspector was explaining everything, the last masked man pushed the inspector to shoot at Alisha, but another inspector pushed him, and he missed the shot, but the bullet hit Mr. Mehra's arm, and he screamed in pain. More policemen entered and knocked off the shooter. Alisha picked up her phone to call an ambulance, and she escorted Mr. Mehra to the hospital and informed his family. The policemen nabbed all four of them. Amravati cried over the phone and gave her address to the police for protection from honor killing.

A Few Days Later

"Hello, Doctor Alisha. Thanks for caring for my father," said a voice.

Alisha turned and saw Vaastu standing behind her.

"Mr. Mehra is your father. Why didn't I notice his resemblance to you? I never thought of meeting you this way. Armed men had entered my clinic today and tried to shoot me but missed, and the bullet struck your father. I am sorry, Vaastu. I wanted to ensure that he was fine, so I escorted him to the hospital. Now you have come, so I can leave. Where is your wife?"

"Thanks for taking care of my father. I am divorced. It is a long story. I will tell you if you want to know. In short, she left me for another guy. She felt our romance died after our son was born," said Vaastu leaning on a pillar.

"Sorry to hear."

"What about you? Did you marry Ashok or someone else?" he asked.

"I am married to Ashok. My parents were looking for a well-settled guy, and Ashok matched all parameters. I had no choice, and now after five years, we are standing here facing each other again. I had never expected this day in my life as you left me after Ashok proposed to me in front of the whole college. He showered petals from the sky. Everyone was in awe except me. Somewhere I felt Ashok was not right for me. But for five years, we have been married and busy with our careers and have less time with each other.

"I am sorry. Your yes broke my heart, and from that day, I left you not expecting to meet you like this because of my father. One of my friends took my dad to your clinic. Thanks for helping him and making him come out from our loss," said Vaastu looking closely at Alisha. She had not changed a bit in those four years except her eyes lacked liveliness. Her beautiful long hair complemented her height. While Vaastu was lost looking at her thinking if he still had a chance, Alisha's phone rang.

"What's wrong Anupama? Why are you crying?"

"Madam, I saw Ashok Sir kissing a pregnant woman in his car which was parked in your building's parking lot two days ago. I followed his car in an auto, and his car stopped inside the parking lot of a luxury apartment. I was stopped by a guard outside that apartment. He asked me why I was following him, and I told him that he is someone else's husband. He laughed at me and said that I must have mistaken him for someone else as that woman and Ashok Sir have been a couple for three long years. They also have a kid, and she is expecting again. The worst part is that she is just 19 years old, and her first child was born when she was seventeen. I couldn't gather the courage to tell you all this," said Anupama sobbing, and my phone fell from my hand. I fell on the ground unable to withstand Ashok's betrayal and that too for a teenager whom he married and made pregnant against the law. I was wondering whom I had married.

Vaastu instantly came by my side and asked, "What's wrong? Did something bad happen?"

I had no courage left in me as my world had turned upside down, but he held me close, and I burst into tears.

SCREWED UP

5th March 2522

7:30 am

"This is Jonathan reporting on duty, Mr. Hans. The news I bring is not good."

"Don't waste words," said Mr. Hans.

"Everyone is dead at your laboratory in Taiwan. The brutality of this mass massacre cannot be stated in words. I froze and took an hour to catch my breath and senses," informed Jonathan.

"Call the police while I try to reach the Prime Minister's office for all needed help," instructed Hans.

Within 10 minutes, the police had arrived and found a blood-soaked floor with dead bodies thrown all around.

"Did you see anyone leaving, Jonathan?" asked Inspector Peter, trying to keep his eyes off the inhumaneness.

"No, Sir. But I called other security staff before calling Mr. Hans. They are still cold. I have puked multiple times and still feel queasiness in my stomach."

"We must seal this area. Nobody can come inside," ordered the Inspector.

"Sorry to interrupt, Inspector Peter, but I need some data to save more lives in this city," said Hans, smoking a traditional cigar.

"Save more lives?" asked Peter in surprise.

"Here is my additional team who were working on a drug to strengthen and regenerate muscles and bones. They believe that after five shots on our testing samples, they broke out of the laboratory, and while our staff and security tried to stop them, they killed them," replied Hans, puffing his cigar.

"Do you see these dead bodies? Can you realize the viciousness? How can your trial specimen be this powerful? Which animals were being used for this?" asked Peter, pointing around.

"We have many tests and vaccine developments going on in this facility, and we have been in this business for two centuries. Our Quantum Artificial Intelligence is much more advanced than any laboratory in the world. Our experiments use advanced quantum cellular medicine that can disable our specimen with just a click. So kindly allow my researchers and technicians to do their job," replied Hans.

"You haven't answered me yet. Which animals were you experimenting on? They tore the bellies apart and ate it. I haven't seen such a case in my entire 15 years of my career," said Peter.

"We were experimenting on human bodies," replied Bo with great pride.

"I don't find you speaking sense. These can only be done by your laboratory-created Chimppards, which are a mixed breed of chimpanzees and leopards. We can't leave them in the wild because of their speed and ferociousness. How can a dead human body do this?" said Peter, making a face as if he ate an Italian ice that had snow crab mixed in it for breakfast, spoiling his day.

"Let's go inside, and we will explain to you," said Bo, trying to sympathize with him.

"What kind of people are you? Your own people are lying dead here, and you are trying to sympathize with me. I don't understand if what is roaming free is more dangerous or you guys," said Peter in disbelief.

Chao came forward and escorted Peter inside while his team was noting everything and sealing that area. They entered the laboratory, which had been shattered, and one unit got down to the task of fixing it. Chao, Bo, Scot, Fai, Hans, Peter, and Tim moved ahead to reach the alternate laboratory and started checking the footage from last night. At one instance, Bo screamed in horror, and Peter interrupted, "This is worse than the 'Last of the Vampire' movie that was recently released, in which humans ate the vampires."

"I didn't realize that five doses of A5-Re-Bon25 could be so potent. When we quantum-simulated the fifth dose in the specimens, we didn't anticipate this outcome. How could this happen? It is impossible," said Fai, touching unconventional quantum reality like a pro, matching codes and sequences on the virtual screen.

"How is this possible? Did someone disturb the delicate entanglement?" asked Scot, carefully analyzing the results.

"You mean we injected another specimen," said Chao, scrolling through the list.

"Who messed up?" asked Hans, and everyone seemed clueless.

"People who knew are no more. Let's check the system memory for clues," said Bo, and her robotic fingers moved faster than ancient spaceships.

"There has been a disaster. The specimen had been injected into brain regenerative bodies. Can you see the results? Their brains were more functional than normal human brains. We will have to deactivate quantum brain chips planted in their brains. This will deactivate them, and we can bring them back to our lab," suggested Bo.

"You experimented on live human bodies. Did you have permission for the same?" asked Peter, stepping back while searching for his immobilizing gun.

"They were bodies of brain-dead people who reached our lab within an hour. We can keep such bodies alive for years as their other organs are functional. We were trying to find cures for all sorts of mental illnesses through this brain regenerative procedure. Somebody intentionally injected A5-Re-Bon25 into them. But the point is that it went unnoticed even after five injections in this brain regenerative specimen. How? Did our enemy alien planets hack into our system and switch the specimen?" remarked Scot and opened the list of scientists working on that project.

"How many of them are alive?" asked Peter, reviewing and noting the names to match the list of the dead outside.

"We want the dead bodies of our people. We will see if we can make them alive again," said Hans, moving to and fro around that place.

"You want to play with nature's laws. You want to keep the dead alive with your bloody science. Do you realize the cost that we will have to pay for it?" yelled Peter.

"We have successfully achieved this by mistake or maybe by a deliberate effort who could foresee the trial of this experiment. I can't lose a bunch of brilliant minds," emphasized Hans while sitting comfortably on a virtual chair.

"Check the location of our specimen. They are hungry and might be looking for food and…," said Chao, and Peter interrupted him, "What do you plan to do with your dead scientists and workers' bodies?"

"Last night we received a hundred brain-dead bodies. I was thinking that we could replace their brains with our people's brains and restore their long-term memories so that they can return to their families, though in a different body. There will be no loss to anyone. Same thoughts and emotions. Moreover, they can be part of our team again like before," said Scot and started to run programs to perform multiple robotic brain surgeries with immediate effect.

"We have a process to follow. You can't do it immediately," said Peter, checking the status of this massacre on his phone.

"Connect me to PM's office. I will take his approval for this trial and save innocent lives. I also want to know who had run this trial," ordered Hans, and Chao resumed work.

In a few minutes, approval had been granted, but police officers had to be kept in the loop.

10:30 am

After an hour of operation, the open skulls were efficaciously closed. Monitoring of the system showed positive results.

"Congratulations! Our experiment shows a 99% success rate," said Tim, scrolling down the screen.

"I have some disturbing news," said Fai, rushing near the operation room.

"Did you make ghosts alive?" asked Peter.

"Nope. Worse," replied Fai and showed us the count of missing specimens, which was a hundred times more than the actual count, increasing every minute.

"How is this possible?" asked Chao bewildered.

"Did you resurrect the dead also?" asked Tim, trying to peel the skin off his eyes to ensure he wasn't in 'The Good Place'.

"Guys, it is worse," said Fai, clicking on the profile locations of the resurrected ones.

"What can be worse than this?" asked Bo shockingly, and Peter commented, "Didn't know that you guys also have an emotion called fear. I thought it was for mortals like us."

"Dead have resurrected dead," said Fai, almost running out of breath.

"Somebody discovered a way to bring back the dead, or did they discover an asexual reproduction technique directly to adulthood in a few minutes?" asked Hans, staring at the quantum data on the invisible ginormous screen.

"It's worse. Thousands of our chips are missing from the lab. But we didn't produce so many. Who did it and carried it with them? What will they do with it?" searched Scot, looking carefully at every piece of information flashing on the screen.

"I doubt asexual reproduction but decoherence has a high possibility. Who could do this? Why can't I find the source of betrayal?" said Chao, working closely with his colleague Scot.

"Hunt for photons and scan stored memory information before arriving at any conclusion," ordered Tim, who was hacking into our enemy's alien planet's data.

"Are you nuts? You have a police officer standing next to you, and you are fearlessly hacking into Eguanta's system," yelled Hans, rushing towards him.

Tim continued, "Ethical hacking. It's an ancient term, but some people still have it in their dictionary, boss. Don't panic as you are not in the red zone yet...," "Or maybe you are now. They are trying to hack our system, superseding our state," stammered Scot with his fingers running faster than Usain Bolt.

"We have entered their system, and I am downloading their research history. Scot, block them from downloading our research menace," bawled Tim while Bo and Fai started to match their research history with ours, prompting the system to beep.

"I found it, but maybe we have alerted them. Don't freak out with the results," declared Fai, pointing at the highlighted data file 'Mission Earth'.

"What is it? It dates back fifty years ago. What does it have in store for us?" asked Hans, conscience-stricken while trying to read the alien coded message with great difficulty, and Chao came to his rescue, who was the decoding expert reading the message aloud, "Mission aborted due to sudden murder of our accomplice. The mission will start after Brandon Senior is alive again."

Listening to that name, Hans ran towards the screen to get a closer look at it and remarked, "I know this guy. He was about to destroy our planet by selling our freedom to them. We would have been slaves of these Eguantans if it would not be for my aunt who lost her life in this fight to save our planet."

Everyone in the room looked unbelievably at Hans, who was a man of few words for a better explanation. He continued, "My uncle Brandon Senior was married to my aunt Lisa. My aunt had given birth to twins Palo and Bae. She was on cloud earth when the news of treachery broke her happiness. Brandon was dating Marla, the princess of Eguanta. Aunt Lisa confronted him asking what he found attractive in that two-legged iguana resembling a human body with a tail. His answer robbed her peace," and silence filled that space.

"Did he want to leave your aunt?" asked Bo sympathetically.

"Yes, but he didn't mention the true reason which she later discovered about his fantasy of ruling Earth. It all started so soon. I still remember that day when I came to the lab with my father when the deal was being signed," said Hans and heaved a sigh of relief.

"Why wasn't it documented? Why was the evidence destroyed?" interrupted Tim.

"It was for the world to not know and sleep peacefully without the fear of our alien neighbours attacking us. Eguanta and Lotusland were in this together. Eguanta's knowledge and Lotusland's magic together were no match for us. They would have wiped the whole planet in just a blink. It took us a lot of effort to convince Lotusland to help us in our fight against Eguanta, which they did but at the cost of human sacrifice. My aunt Lisa and her kids Palo and Bae had to pay the cost of Brandon's deeds," answered Hans, and Peter was documenting it all the way. "This is personal. Please don't document it," requested Hans, and Peter smiled, saying that he was doing his duty.

Hans continued: "The world that we see today was very different 50 years ago. Earth was at war with all the neighbouring planets for survival due to a sudden climatic change that was sucking life from it to keep itself alive. The decomposed dead bodies were keeping Earth alive as the atmosphere was changing molecules into oxygen. So, for abundant oxygen, more dead bodies. This was the result of our war with Mada Vegas, whose advanced molecular life sciences had made it inhabitable after we captured their queen. They released biomolecules into our atmosphere, which reversed our ecosystem, causing millions to die to sustain our planet. At this rate, humans were on the verge of extinction. We called out for help. Eguanta and Lotusland came to restore our planet, and it is then Brandon met Marla. Lisa had noticed the spark between them and objected to their official meeting without others involved."

"Why didn't her father object to their closeness?" asked Peter.

"Marcus was in love with Lotusland's princess, Percy, who loved Derick. Her father, Christopher, magical weapons were designed by Derick. Those events are still fresh in my memory lane," said Hans.

"The point is that it is history. Right now, stop deep artificial neural learning for complex systems. All these specimens will be deactivated. This fifty-year-old human specimen system will stop and drop dead forever. We will destroy them and build new systems from scratch. It's time to rewrite history and bring justice for my aunt. Brandon cannot resurrect the dead," further said Hans.

THOSE DARK GREEN EYES

3rd May 2012, Bozhentsi

Bozhentsi being an architectural reserve and part of UNESCO's cultural monuments to protect it from construction with a handful of houses was one of my favourite spots for spending my time away from my strenuous job as a general surgeon in Bulgaria. I was there to spend three nights alone in an empty guest house. I had been in Gabrovo to treat a teenage boy who had met with an unfortunate accident and a part of his brain had been affected due to traumatic brain injury (TBI). Along with medication, I decided to try deep brain stimulation (DBS) on that boy. Although this treatment may be risky at times but in his case, it worked miraculously. To destress myself I came to this small village, Bozhentsi and watched fire dance where my eyes met a dancer's dark green eyes. I was unable to take off my eyes from that teenage girl and was curiously watching her. I looked good on paper but when it came to asking out, I would speak heebie-jeebies and no girl would come with me. I somewhere knew that luck and misfortune are intertwined but was a strong disbeliever of this theory. My relationship with my profession was no happy accident. My brother was a rash driver and met with an accident that left half of his body paralyzed. Adversity didn't strike my family with instructions and remedies in hand. This incident shook me as an adolescent and since then my struggle to find a silver lining started.

My success at the age of twenty-five was envied by many as they were unaware of the misfortune behind my Midas touch. I started my first trial of my brother somewhere beyond medical ethics to make him stand on his two feet with support. I made sure that I visited my family once a month but right now I was watching a Bulgarian beauty playing with fire. My heart was picking pace on her fiery moves and music, nor did people seem to matter other than that teenage girl. I was somewhat ashamed for feeling that way but still couldn't stop myself. It felt like a signal of God.

I asked myself, "Are you sure about it?"

I heard the reply echoing in that crowded place, "Not sure," as it was summer, and my nieces might be at my family home for their summer vacation. They were a little younger than this girl who had spiked my oxytocin.

In this dreamy stretch of time, I missed out on the detail when she fell on the ground with a fire burning around. Her troupe was rescuing her and in no time, she was far away from fire. Her cat eyes and golden hair seemed lifeless. I lost a beat and ran to the spot closely examining her pulse rate and heartbeat when I heard a woman saying, "What do you think you are doing?"

"My duty."

"Who do you think you are?" she further questioned.

This time I looked at her calmly and answered, "A doctor. So now let me examine the patient."

There was silence and I could hear her sinking heartbeat without a stethoscope.

Scared of wasting a second, I said, "I must take her to the hospital. Her condition is not good. The ambulance will take time to reach here so I am taking her in my car."

I couldn't believe it myself. Was I out of my mind? She could lose her life on the way to the hospital. I should have called an ambulance but like a love-stricken dove, I was ready to take this career-threatening risk. I was wondering how much worse it could be for a brain surgeon visiting an emotional counsellor for his hijacked heart that propelled him for escorting this seductress.

I refused to argue with myself, so I hastily said, "Are there any acquaintances?" while praying for none.

"No," said the woman.

I tried to move her hands and limbs to check for any signs of partial consciousness, but she remained unresponsive. Without a second thought, I pinched her hard, and she took a long breath.

"Help me take her to the car and please inform her family," I said, giving the woman a business card with the hospital's name.

Although I had many business cards due to my association with several hospitals, this time I was only carrying one. The lady and some locals helped me place the girl in my car, and I emphasized, "I need at least one of her family members in my hospital. Make it soon."

"That girl, Victoria, has only one family member," said the woman.

I wasn't expecting this green-eyed girl to have just one family member. My heart raced as I thought about my own family and thanked my stars for blessing me with a long list of extended family members.

I decided to take the shortest route, Route 5524 and Route 5, to cover the almost 16 km journey in thirty minutes, even though having a sinking patient in the backseat made it feel longer.

Upon reaching Gabrovo, I heaved a sigh of relief and quickly headed for the hospital. The hospital staff saw my car with the patient in the back seat, and they immediately brought a stretcher and a drip. I signaled for an oxygen cylinder, and they obliged. Doctors and interns approached me, eager to know the condition of Victoria.

"I want her MRI and CT scan reports," I instructed the nurse and junior doctors.

In seconds, the team got down to work, and I took the opportunity to visit my other patients to check on their developments.

"Dr. Hristo, there is someone here to meet you," called out Elena, the receptionist.

I hadn't realized that more than an hour had passed since I started visiting and talking to my patients. I went to my cabin and found a middle-aged lady sitting there.

"How can I help you?" I asked.

"I am Victoria's mother," she said nervously.

I politely asked, "Did you fill out the form?"

"Yes. Is my daughter fine?" Maria, Victoria's mother, replied.

"For how long has this episode been going on?"

"She has fainted a couple of times, but never for this long. I am worried for her," said Maria, her voice breaking as she wept.

"Is she on any medications?"

"Not yet. I thought her anxiety would settle with time. It started soon after I found her in the fields half-naked. When I asked her what happened, she didn't remember anything. Forgetting things has been common for her, and these episodes became more frequent after her father died. Victoria helps me with odd jobs to support us," Maria explained, still crying.

"Do you know that she has been having short episodes of stroke?"

"No," Maria replied, starting to cry again.

"Is there any history of mental illness in your family?"

"Not much, other than the fact that I take anti-depressants to help with smiling and sleeping. Victoria is not taking any medication as of now," Maria responded.

"Do you know that your daughter is pregnant?" I managed to say with wobbly lips.

Maria gasped, and I could relate to her shock. Although I had heard about teenage pregnancies, this was the first case I had personally encountered. It was too early to declare a broken heart, but I couldn't help feeling a gloomy smile creeping onto my face.

"She is under observation. It might take hours, days, or even months. Do you know who the father is? We have two lives to save."

"I have no clue. Maybe Victoria knows," said Maria.

"Did she tell you anything about it?"

"No," she replied.

"Then maybe she doesn't know herself."

"You are right. She is just 16 years old and forgets important things. I should have been more careful," she said, crying.

"Did she have any boyfriends?"

"No. We were so engrossed in earning our living that she didn't have any friends, even in school. I can't imagine her being involved with someone intimately," said Maria, her voice trembling.

"In that case, we must register a police complaint. The culprit is absconding, and your daughter is suffering."

"I can't file a police complaint. Victoria is already in shock, and you are advising me to do something unthinkable. How can a mother do that to her own daughter?" said Maria, raising her voice so that she could be heard.

"What do you want then?"

"Victoria had a boyfriend. How could I forget? She mentioned it a few times. But he left the village to pursue his studies. She told me that she was expecting but didn't want to stop Daniel from pursuing his dreams for a better future. As you mentioned, she might have forgotten those moments due to her illness and might not want to keep the baby. So please, do whatever you can to ensure that my daughter is fine. I am poor and will not be able to support the baby. Help me find a foster home for her baby," Maria pleaded, folding her hands.

"How will you pay for the hospital bills?"

"I don't know. Maybe I can work in this hospital to pay the bills," she replied, hopeful.

"Even if we waive off half of the fees because you are working here, you will still have significant expenses," I explained.

She looked at me with pleading eyes as if shaking my soul to show some humanity.

“Fine. You start working here in the housekeeping department and I will take care of the rest.”

One Week Later

“How is Victoria’s progress?” I asked my team of doctors.

"Same. But we are hopeful. Due to her pregnancy, things have become complicated," replied Dr. Nikolas.

I looked closely at her, searching for any sign of response. Her dark green eyes were tightly shut, and tears started to flow down my cheeks. To avoid an embarrassing moment, I quickly left the room, but Victoria remained on my mind. I had decided not to charge Maria anything for the treatment, and I was visiting the hospital every week to closely monitor her daughter's progress. However, despite our efforts, we were unsure why Victoria wasn't responding. Maria stayed in the hospital to be near her daughter and worked tirelessly to pay the mounting bills and save her.

One Month Later

"The baby seems to be fine. This means that Victoria is fighting for life."

"Yes, doctor. We feel the same. The only worrying part is that she is still not awake. It is quite possible that we will have to deliver the child earlier than the due date," said Dr. Nikolas as he went through Victoria's reports.

"Do you have anything to say, Dr. Ivanka?"

"I agree with Dr. Nikolas. Victoria has not yet come out of her vegetative state. I am concerned about both the mother and the child. It feels strange to call a sixteen-year-old girl a mother, but we must accept the facts. Delivering a child in a vegetative state at this tender age won't be easy. I am just praying that she wakes up soon," said Dr. Ivanka, carefully examining Victoria and the growing child inside her.

I stood there, looking at her pale face and immobile body, hoping that she would miraculously wake up. At night, Maria slept in her daughter's room, and she always thanked me for helping them whenever we met. Although I was drawn to Victoria, I was not prepared to act on these feelings, especially in this difficult situation. Despite her being near me, it felt more like a collaborative telepresence than a warm, comforting connection. She made me feel like a teenager again, and even in the stressful work environment, she had a way of making me feel alive and vibrant. I did everything in my power to keep her alive and give her the best possible chance for recovery.

Three weeks later

"Dr. Hristo, can you come over to the hospital now? Victoria is responding. She opened her eyes, but she is still not speaking," said Nurse Amelia over the phone.

"She opened her eyes."

These four words echoed in my ears. Checking my watch, it was 8 pm, but I decided to drive to Gabrovo immediately to see Victoria. I grabbed my coat and rushed to the parking lot, desperate to have a heart-to-heart connection with her. All the way, I couldn't stop thinking about Victoria, wondering if she had noticed me that night and if she remembered me at all. A doctor thinking about a teenage patient in this way seemed cynical, but when it came to matters of the heart, the brain didn't function rationally. This stupefied feeling was driving me crazy, but it was not something I could prescribe as a remedy.

I arrived at Victoria's hospital room, but I couldn't take a step inside the door. I saw her looking around, surrounded by my team of doctors. Her dark green eyes seemed confused, searching for answers. Maria was sitting beside her daughter, holding her hand.

"She is responding. We can't reveal her pregnancy. Her reaction to the pregnancy can be unpredictable and might send her into a state of shock again," said Dr. Ivanka, and I couldn't have agreed more.

I nodded and approached Victoria to see her eyes alive and awake. Before I could say anything, she softly said, "You brought me here," and I whispered, "Yes," into her ears.

The nearness made my heart leap with joy, but I left to have a conversation with Dr. Ivanka.

"I think Victoria should be put on sedatives, and her pregnancy must not be disclosed. It will be good for her recovery."

"I agree," said Dr. Ivanka, and we designed a three-month recovery plan, keeping both mother and baby in mind.

I decided to visit Victoria every week to chat with her and forget myself for some time.

Two months later

"Dr. Ivanka, hurry! Victoria is losing consciousness again. Her heartbeat is sinking," said Amelia, interrupting our conversation.

"We will have to operate on Victoria. It's early, but we can't take the chance. Amelia, immediately make the operation theatre ready," said Dr. Ivanka, and I hurriedly left to check on Victoria, hoping that everything would be fine.

The next two hours were critical as we tried to stabilize both the mother and the child. Her son was taken to the neo-natal care, and Victoria was under observation. Maria saw the baby who had inherited Victoria's dark green eyes. He looked like a mini replica of Victoria, and I couldn't stop myself from looking at him.

Maria came dashing into my room and said, "It's difficult for me, but I want to put the newborn up for adoption after he is completely healthy. It will be best for Victoria. Will you help me?" She looked at me with pleading eyes.

"Don't worry. It will be done."

For a few days, I stayed in Gabrovo to ensure that my heart-to-heart connection was not broken, and it paid off. In a span of three months, Victoria had recovered, and she was prescribed medication for a year to fully recover. Before her discharge from the hospital, she came to meet me. As she entered my room, I was captivated by her presence.

"My mother told me what you did to save me. How can I repay you?" she asked.

I walked closer to her, gently touching her golden-brown hair, and without hesitation, kissed her on her cheeks.

She stepped back and said, "This is not possible. I am not prepared to be your girlfriend. I have a lot on my plate. I want to finish my studies and then work. You don't fit into my plans. But I will surely return your money. Please don't misunderstand me. I really like you, but now is not the right time."

Tears rolled down my cheeks, and words got stuck in my mouth. After minutes of silence, she left, and I felt my heart shatter.

"Did you miss the boat?" asked Dr. Ivanka, giving me a wake-up call. I looked at her like a lifeless turnip, unable to respond. Last night she didn't let me leave her room, and now she didn't let me kiss her. I kept asking myself how to forget this night, the first night of my life.

"I heard that Victoria's child has been adopted. I met the NGO's director yesterday regarding one of my cases," said Dr. Ivanka.

"That's nice."

"I also came to know that you are shifting permanently to Sofia, your hometown. Why so hastily?" she further inquired.

In great pain, I murmured, "I need them," and then left with my belongings.

Ten Years Later

"Earlier, you were never on time. Last night you chose not to come. What's going on with you, Hristo? Do you realize that we are getting married?" said Albena, annoyed with my sullen attitude.

Her words seemed to fall on deaf ears, and she picked up her jacket, muttering, "As if trying to convince this lady to forget about her dead mother's last wish isn't driving me crazy, and now you're here to add to my pain."

"Dead mother?" I finally spoke up.

"The dragon's mouth opens! Dr. Johnson referred a special case. The young lady is going through a painful divorce. Her billionaire husband cheated on her with multiple women. She has a daughter who refuses to stay with her father. Before she died, her mother informed her that she also has a son, without revealing any details. Now this lady wants to search for her imaginary son and complicate her divorce even further," Albena explained as she moved towards the door.

I swiftly stood up and held her by her waist.

"Hold your horses, doctor. What's gotten into you?" she asked suspiciously.

"Nothing. We are going out for dinner tonight. I'm sorry for keeping you waiting last night," I replied.

Albena stared at me, unconvinced, and said, "You liar. Come on, spit it out." I playfully dragged her out for dinner.

Throughout the evening, she leaned on my shoulder, but my mind was preoccupied with the term "Dead mother."

The Chinese restaurant we went to was surprisingly busy even on a Wednesday.

I signaled the waiter for a corner table with candles, surprising Albena with my romantic gesture. She asked, "Are you alright?"

"What makes you think I'm not?" I replied.

"Ask yourself. When have you ever booked a table for the two of us?" she inquired.

I smiled at her, though my mind was scheming on how to accidentally knock over a glass of water on our table - "BAAM" - and I did it.

"Oh, dear. I'm sorry," I apologized.

"Hristo, you're worse than a kid," she said angrily, then went to the ladies' washroom to fix her dress and appearance.

As I sat there, I wondered how kids could be worse, considering I was the father of a ten-year-old. In our five years of relationship, Albena never spoke of having kids of our own. Sometimes she would babysit Velyo, but mostly I had to leave him with my parents. This often made Velyo sad, but I tried to compensate by giving him expensive gifts and taking him on family vacations to resorts.

Surprisingly, I had started to question the very understanding between Albena and myself.

It occurred to me that I had not yet checked Albena's phone for her patients' appointment list. She marked her appointments on Google Calendar with a brief patient description.

The next minute, my robotic hands were scrolling down the list, and my X-ray eyes were scanning the details to store them in my computerized memory.

"Why are you checking my calendar?" Albena asked, touching my shoulder.

"I'm looking at it to see if you have any appointments on a special day next month," I replied.

"Why?"

"You again forgot my son's birthday."

"Oh, Hristo, I'm sorry. I know you have hectic schedules, and yet you manage time for Velyo. I'm also trying," she said, kissing me.

"Yeah, I know. You've been trying sincerely for the last five years," I said sarcastically.

"Honey, we both have our careers to focus on, and it's difficult to think about having kids. I'm happy the way we are and would like it to be the same for two more years," she explained.

"This is the same statement I hear every single year. You'll never change, Albena."

"I am still the same, but you have changed," she said, looking at me questionably.

"Why don't you invite all your patients you are meeting on Velyo's birthday to my place instead of not attending my son's birthday? What will I tell my family?" I asked.

"Okay, now don't get angry. My assistant will personally call them and invite them to your countryside farmhouse. Does that make you happy?" she suggested.

I remained silent. Suddenly, this argument made me forget about Victoria. I had adopted her son, Velyo. I raised him like my own, keeping Victoria's memory alive through his dark green eyes.

"Whom am I fooling?" I thought to myself.

After Victoria joined an airline company, I lost track of her. She used to travel a lot, and I left it up to destiny. However, just seeing the name "Victoria" on Albena's phone made me decide to invite all her patients to my son's birthday party. I knew it would be crowded, but I couldn't wait to solve the mystery of Victoria's life.

Velyo's Birthday

“Mom, the arrangement looks cozy and stylish. I don't know what I would do without you."

"Now, you will be a married man, and my responsibilities will shift to Albena's shoulders," said Mom, laughing.

Guests had started to arrive, but there was still no sign of Victoria. It was almost seven, and I couldn't shake off the fear of disappointment. Mom announced for everyone to join in for the cake cutting.

We gathered around the cake like bees around flowers. While everyone was busy singing the "Happy Birthday" song, my eyes were fixed on the door. Velyo turned to offer me a bite of his birthday cake, but I couldn't open my mouth. Victoria was standing at the door with a 9-year-old girl who looked exactly like her. My eyes welled up with tears, like the moist cake.

Surprisingly, everyone was looking at her, and some women moved closer to their partners. Mom noticed me looking at Victoria and pinched me. I looked at her questioningly. The guests got busy chatting and eating, and I snuck out of my family zone to talk to my first love.

"How are you?" I asked Victoria.

She looked at me with wet eyes and said, "It feels nice to see you after so many years. How have you been doing? Did you get married?"

Velyo came running to me and said, "Dad, let's go and eat. I'm hungry," but his broken words were followed by Albena's barrage of questions: "Why does this woman look familiar? Not just familiar, but Velyo is a Xerox copy of this lady. Is she family or something? Why do I feel that we have met before?"

Nobody knew that I was not the biological father of Velyo.

Both Albena and Velyo looked at me expectantly.

Victoria stared at Velyo and gasped. She asked me, "Is he my lost son?"

Albena immediately ran towards our room, and I followed her.

"Albena, you're getting it wrong," I tried to explain.

"What am I getting wrong? Is it your affair with that woman or the fact that Velyo is not your child? What is it? How could you hide it from me? She is my client that I spoke about on our last dinner date. I was a fool. You were dating her too," she shouted angrily.

"You never asked me about Velyo's mother."

"Now she's back in your life, and I'm leaving," she said angrily.

"Albena, you're overreacting. Maybe Hristo was in a relationship with Velyo's mother, but he is marrying you. He loves you, and you can't leave us," said my mother, kissing Albena's forehead.

"Then please tell your son to express his feelings for me," she said.

My mother stared at me, and I got down on one knee, holding a solitaire in my hand, and said, "Victoria, will you marry me?"

Albena hit me on my head with her purse, saying, "Whom are you fooling?"

With tears in my eyes, I looked at her and she stormed out angrily.

Victoria came near me and said, "I'm sorry. I didn't realize that you loved me. I love you too, and my failed marriage was the result of the feelings I had for you. I could never accept Mark as my husband, and after my mother's death, I decided to divorce him."

With tears in my eyes, I asked, "Why did you vanish suddenly?" She replied, "Amanda is your daughter."

I stepped back, asking, "Why didn't you tell me?"

"After I left the hospital, I got an air-hostess job. While travelling, I fell in love with my estranged husband. His eccentricity and charm brought us closer. After a few dates, he proposed to me, and my mother didn't let me refuse. He was a billionaire, and my mom didn't want me to lose this opportunity for a stable life. In my fourth month of pregnancy, we got married, but then we soon found out that I was pregnant. Mark said that he was not the biological father of the child, which confused me as we were dating. He told me that due to a medical condition, he could not father a child. He then asked me whose child I was carrying, and I knew it was yours. But it was too late. He was happy that I was pregnant. Amanda was a symbol of his failure, and our fights increased due to his insecurities, which dragged me to court and a session with your girlfriend Albena. I saw your picture with her on her cell phone last month. I told Mark as he wanted Amanda's custody. He didn't agree. I knew about this party, so I came here to hand over your daughter," said Victoria, lending Amanda's hand towards me.

"Why should I believe you?" I asked, crying while my hands covered my eyes. There was silence in the room, but my weeping could be heard aloud. I raised my head to look at Victoria, but she was not there. I ran out to ask why she left without her daughter, but Albena stopped me and said, "I received a call from the police station inquiring about one of my clients who died last night."

I immediately stopped to listen, and she continued, "That client's name is Victoria. I informed them that they were wrong as she is here in our holiday home with her daughter to attend our son's birthday party. He said that he is sending me pictures and news of her death. Also, he will be coming to my office to inquire about her patient history to know who murdered her, as her estranged husband was not in town."

"Victoria left. I was going out to look for…," I stammered, and my eyes stopped on the picture of a dead Victoria.

We both ran inside to talk to Amanda, who was still standing where I had left her.

Albena went near her and asked, "Where are your mother and father?"

Amanda looked surprised and said, "In a fight last night with my father, Mom pushed him from our balcony on the fourth floor, and he fell into the lake. She then took me to bed and promised that we will go to meet my real father tomorrow."

"Where were you when your parents were fighting?"

"I was cuddling my teddy bear in my room," she replied.

Albena's phone rang, and it was the same policeman.

The inspector said, "Surprisingly, your client's husband was in town, and we have recovered his dead body from the lake. We still don't know who murdered them as their daughter is missing," and Albena said, "Amanda is here with us."

There was silence over the phone, and Inspector Rodrick said that he was coming over to meet her.

I hugged Amanda and asked, "Where is your mother?"

"Mark tried to kill her with a knife. She fell on the kitchen floor, and the knife was pierced in her belly. He was then coming towards me with another knife, but then my mother came from behind and dragged him towards the balcony and threw him out. She then took me to bed, and I slept with my teddy," replied Amanda.

"Was she hurt?" asked Albena, and her reply shook us, "No. But she was sad and said that she has to leave soon."

I ran outside and saw Victoria's car parked outside my holiday home. I searched for her all around but couldn't find her anywhere. Albena called up the inspector to register a missing complaint for Victoria, but he informed her that both the dead bodies were in the post-mortem room. This was my first vacation with my family in my holiday home to reconnect with them and feel life other than my social responsibility. Everyone was happy until Victoria arrived and left Amanda behind. Albena held my hand, comforting me that she was there by my side, but I knew somewhere that those dark green eyes would haunt me my entire life.